Metaphorosis

December 2022

Beautifully made speculative fiction

Also from Metaphorosis

Metaphorosis

December 2022

edited by
B. Morris Allen

ISSN: 2573-136X (online)
ISBN: 978-1-64076-242-8 (e-book)
ISBN: 978-1-64076-243-5 (paperback)

Metaphorosis
a magazine of speculative fiction

from
Metaphorosis Publishing

Neskowin

December 2022

The Dragon's Due

Christopher Warden

The dragon dove out of the sky, claws extended, ready to strike. Its scales flashed so brightly in the morning sun that it hurt my eyes. As it landed, claws still out, jaws agape, I wondered if it might grab me. Pinned by its claws, its fangs would rip me in two with ease. Or perhaps it would roast me alive, the smoke hopefully suffocating me before the flames blistered my skin off. Either way, it would be a serious violation of the rules.

The dragon had size and strength, fangs and claws, fire and flight. I had the rules. That and my brains. It hardly seemed enough.

Fortunately, dragons are not fools (unlike many of the people I work for). True, it wanted to eat me, but one human cannot feed a dragon. One human is an appetizer. Dragons need lots of people, a whole kingdom of people, or in this case, a duchy.

But even a duchy is not enough. If a dragon hunts any area at will, it will deplete the human population in a matter of months. After that, it must move on, often into another dragon's territory, which means they fight. That causes huge fires and massive destruction. It's a nightmare, with towns and farmland destroyed: chaos, exodus, and plague — things that neither dragons nor people want.

Hunter and prey both need a more stable solution. That's where I come in.

The dragon settled down on the hillside slightly above me. It had claimed the higher ground, always a shrewd tactic. It stretched its great wings once, almost like a yawn, then curled its tail around its massive frame and settled its head upon the ground. It peered at me, and I could see my reflection in its eyes.

I smiled, took a breath, and began my spiel.

"An honor to make your acquaintance," I said, bowing. I always bow at the start. Dragons, like nobles, like it. "As you know," I said, trying to appear calm, "I am here representing the local Duke to negotiate a four-year contract regarding your food supply."

I've personally never liked the term 'food supply', but the other options are even less appetizing: 'human death toll' is too prejudicial, 'deliveries' too commercial, 'bounty' too bucolic, 'morsels' too light-hearted, and 'quota' too antiseptic.

The dragon said nothing to my opening; it was still eyeing me, making me feel like a leg of juicy spit-roasted lamb. Had I misjudged the situation? Would it just eat me? Yes, there would be repercussions for such an act, but that would be little comfort to me as I was being digested in its stomach. I swallowed hard. The dragon was intimidating me, trying to unnerve me. Best to just continue.

"Like all contracts, the agreement we reach will require both parties to make certain...sacrifices." I always like to get that word in: *sacrifice*. It reminds the dragon that lives are at stake. Dragons don't care about human lives, except in terms of quantity, but there's no harm in reminding the dragon that our side does not share its point of view.

It spoke then; its voice was distinctive. Most dragons have unpleasant voices: harsh, gravel-filled growls. Maybe it's all the fire coming out of their throats. This dragon had the voice of a tenor.

"Virgins," it said. "I want virgins."

"Virgins? You're a dragon, not a vampire." I said. "How could virginity make a difference to you?"

"Sex makes human flesh taste sour," it said in its beautiful voice. It almost sounded like a castrato. I wondered if that had something to do with its request, but I wasn't about to ask. *Never piss off the dragon* is the first unwritten rule of my guild.

Then it dawned on me. It didn't want virgins. It wanted young people: tender and succulent like veal. But it knew that would look bad, would cause an uproar — hence the virgin request. Because for some insane reason, that was actually more...palatable?

I almost smiled, but I didn't want to tip my hand.

"You know," I said in an innocent tone, "there's a convent nearby — lots of nuns.

I'm sure they are all virgins, probably eager to be martyrs. I can arrange for a good number of them to come to you."

The dragon growled at that, and I allowed myself a smile at the growl. We both knew that most of the nuns were crones — not the tender meat it was hoping for. And so it was struck by its own lance. Or perhaps burned by its own breath? More importantly, it was something I could leverage.

The dragon glowered at me for a bit, then hissed out two words: "No nuns."

"Well," I said. "If you insist on excluding nuns, it means the total number of victims will have to go down — fair's fair," I said.

I think it almost sighed then.

"How much?" it asked.

And so, we began to haggle over the nun exclusion. The negotiations had begun. An hour later, I had scored my first victory and saved a dozen lives, which not only felt good, but also netted me as many gold coins.

That's how I make my money. Every life I save garners me a coin. The guild determines each territory's projected human-dragon consumption cost, and the assigned negotiator tries to beat that estimate.

I know it sounds cold-blooded, but in my line of work you have to be willing to sell lives to save lives. It's like being a general who needs to take a hill; you know it will cost a certain number of soldiers. You want to make it the smallest number, but it's still going to cost.

"I have yet to see your credentials," the dragon said. It was trying to change the subject and get on a new footing — always a good idea when you've had a setback.

I bowed again and showed my letters of accreditation. My name, Edwin Skein, was emblazoned upon a long vellum scroll in gold ink. The appendices showed a record I was proud of: negotiated settlements with a dozen dragons. My Curriculum Vitae listed my publications in the Journal of Dragon Dealings. I wondered if this dragon had (perhaps in preparation) read any of my writings. Though the guild frowned upon it, it was well known that dragons read the journal; some were so bold as to subscribe.

The negotiations with this dragon, who was named Blood-Wind, (yes, they always have names like that), were grueling. Throughout, its belly rumbled louder and louder. Near the end, it was like a kettle drum beating a march. That was good; it made Blood-Wind eager to conclude the deal. It made me fairly eager also. We had left the hillside and were working in its lair: a many-chambered cave it called Dire-Skull (and yes, they always name their lairs like that too).

After three weeks of haggling, we were ready to lock it up: one thousand eight hundred souls, many taken from local orphanages, to be delivered monthly over four years. The orphanage was a brilliant stroke on my part: young people no one minded parting with. Their inclusion let me shave almost five hundred lives off the deal. I told myself that many of those orphans would have died anyway. The fate of orphans in our modern age is, at best perilous. At least this way, their deaths would save lives. A rationalization, I suppose, but in my line of work, there's a lot of that.

As I tallied the final numbers, I realized this negotiation was a great success. Of course, I would get no thanks.

When a general wins a battle, he's praised. In my case, I'd be called 'ghoul', 'parasite', 'leech', 'traitor', not to my face but behind my back. I would be lumped with the dragon as another monster. It doesn't bother me. Like the dragon, I've grown a tough hide. I'm used to the looks of anger and resentment when I ride into a town. I'm used to eating alone and being served at the back of a hall. I knew what the locals thought about my kind.

But I also knew that this deal was saving lives. In terms of the greater good, this was an excellent arrangement. Between the nuns and the orphans, Nurbleville was getting off light, So I was pleased, even proud of this contract. Then disaster showed up.

Disaster was six foot ten, clad in heavy armor, sitting on the biggest horse imaginable. Disaster was named Sir Granger Goodwin of the Strong Arm. He was blond and blue-eyed and handsome, and he was here to slay the dragon. Just one look at him, and I knew that half the duchy would think he could do it, too.

I was sitting outside at a tavern (alone as usual) enjoying a well-earned celebratory ale when the knight rode in. He went straight to the town square, followed by his squire, a skinny kid on a mule. Sir Goodwin stood up in his stirrups. It made him look like a giant.

The squire pulled out a bugle and blew it until a crowd had formed.

"People of Nurble," Sir Goodwin shouted. "I have come to deliver you from evil. I have come to slay the dragon!"

He swung up his lance. I smiled at that; the symbolism was too much.

"My Lance will pierce the dragon's heart. My aim will be guided by God; all I ask in return are your prayers. Strengthened by your faith, I cannot fail." He was either a terrific liar, a lunatic, or both.

As the crowd grew thicker, Goodwin's description of the slaying of Blood-Wind grew more and more ludicrous. I grew more and more nervous. Fortunately, Duke Nurble arrived. I was relieved to see that Nurble also looked nervous. Nurble was a pragmatic politician. He'd gained his title not by war, but by deft scheming: buying land and shaving coins. He was of the breed of nobility who lived by trade, not sword. Nurble's father had been a pig farmer. The Duke was so modern as to be proud of his father's lowly past: a sow decorated his coat arms. Goodwin, on the other hand, was clearly from an ancient line of warriors.

Despite their differences, the two nobles, astride their horses, leaned towards each other and began to quietly murmur to one another. After a brief exchange, Sir Goodwin turned back to the crowd.

"People of Nurble, I go now to take council with your Duke. Soon, the dragon shall be destroyed; soon, we shall all be rejoicing! Have faith." Then the whole lot of them, knight, Duke, squire, and guards, rode off to the castle.

I followed.

I was on foot, so getting to the Duke's castle took me much longer. Don't imagine some grey fortress when I say castle. The Duke had built a chateau. On arrival, I was taken to the Duke's library: a sad collection of worm-eaten books. It had only three pristine sections: one on pig farming, one on pastry making, and the third (hidden by a false shelf) was made up of cheap erotica mixed with well-thumbed manuals on poisons and soporifics. I'd heard rumors of local maidens disappearing, only to reappear days later with no memory of what had happened to them. The peasants said it was vampires. My contacts in the Undead Umbrage Union had assured me

Nurbleville was vampire-free. Here was the actual answer. Despite my regular dealings with the horrors of my trade, I shuddered. To help take my mind off the matter and help pass the time, I took out one of the pig books.

I did not have to wait long. The Duke came in both smiling and sweating. He looked like a combination of the types of books he kept: a pig eating an eclair stuffed with a filling of hidden toxic obscenity.

"Good news!" he said with an enthusiasm that might have been directed at a piglet about to be slaughtered, a cream puff devoured, or a maiden...well, you get the idea.

"What news, my lord?" I said in as neutral a tone as I could muster.

"Sir Goodwin will slay the dragon in the morning."

I nearly laughed, but instead coughed hard. *Never piss off the nobles* is the second rule of my guild. I stood up and bowed. I had to be careful here. As with dragons, noblemen must be dealt with gingerly. The two have much in common: power, irritability, not to mention terrible breath. This was certainly the case with Duke Nurble. Especially the breath.

"In that case, my services are no longer required," I said.

The Duke looked surprised.

"Sir Goodwin thought you might object," he said.

"Object? What would be the point? I will, however, leave your duchy immediately."

"But you'll miss the victory feast," the Duke said.

"Victory feast?" I asked.

"Yes," he said. "I am told dragon meat is a fine repast: wonderful in meat pies."

I wanted to point out that the business at hand was less like baking pastries and more like making sausage, but I doubted he would get my point.

"No one actually knows what dragon tastes like, my lord," I said. "No one has ever slain a dragon."

"So, you do doubt Sir Goodwin! He told me you would cast doubt upon his valor."

"I am sure he is most valorous, but the dragon is large, fierce, and scaled; it breathes fire and flies. I am not sure that valor will win over all that. And after the battle, the dragon's wrath will be great."

"You assume Sir Goodwin will fail," the Duke said.

"A safe assumption," I said.

"It was Sir Goodwin who defeated that giant to the North," the Duke said.

This took me aback a bit. I had heard through my friends in the Behemoth Bargainer's Brotherhood that the Giant of Bungbole had been slain. So it had been Sir Goodwin who'd (literally) killed Robert Red-Nose's negotiations.

Was it possible? I wondered.

"A giant, while formidable, is no dragon," I said.

"Sir Goodwin has slain a dragon," the Duke said triumphantly.

"Well, he claims he has. My guild keeps close ties regarding all draconic matters. The consequences of such a deed would have reverberated throughout the kingdom."

"It did not happen in the kingdom," a new voice interjected. Hunched in the doorway, looking more giant than ever, was Sir Goodwin. He strode in, his spurs chinking, and threw a gauntlet down on the table. For a moment, I thought he was challenging me to a duel, but then I looked more closely at the gauntlet. It was greenish and scaled: dragon skin.

To my credit, I did not gasp.

"I was on crusade in the East when I came upon the beast," Sir Goodwin said.

19

His face lost all expression, his voice distant and hushed as if he were telling a holy parable, though one involving massive bloodshed.

"Go on, the Duke said. "Tell him!"

The knight nodded; he needed no encouragement.

"To be fair," Sir Goodwin said, "it was old, old even for a dragon, so perhaps not as formidable as the beast I will slay tomorrow, but it was a dragon. I rode away at first, then spun and charged. Before it could react, I struck. My lance found its heart. No doubt God was with me that day. I skinned it and made these gloves and a gambeson for myself and my steed; they resist all fire. The flames of dragons cannot touch me."

"Tell him about the blood!" the Duke blurted.

Sir Goodwin smiled. "After I slew the dragon, I cut out its heart and drank its lifeblood. Since then, I have been blessed with remarkable strength of limb."

The Duke tittered. Nurble was like a love-smitten maiden or a bully's toady. The Duke pulled out a piece of twisted metal from his purse and threw it down next to the gauntlet. It was, or rather had been, a horseshoe; it was now nearly straight. Sir Goodwin picked it up and twisted it back into a U-shape. It was like watching a child bend a green willow reed. The Duke clapped his hands in delight.

My blood ran cold. It was worse than I had thought. Sir Goodwin wasn't just some oversized lunatic. He was the authentic item, an actual slayer of dragons, a figure from legend, a hero. There is nothing, and I mean nothing, more dangerous than a hero. They bring ruin and disaster. There are whole guild treatises written about how to deal with heroes, all of them useless. I had been fearful before; now, I was near panic, but I kept my face motionless.

"Remarkable," I said. "You are to be commended, good sir knight."

Sir Goodwin beamed. "I go now to pray in the Duke's chapel. I will keep vigil there and take midnight mass. On the morrow, with my soul refreshed, I will kill the dragon." He turned and left, spurs still clinking.

When I could no longer hear the jingling of his spurs, I turned to the Duke.

Before I could speak, the Duke cut me off.

"I will not hear any attacks against that man," he said.

I paused. I couldn't stop Sir Goodwin by myself. Dragons I could handle, but a hero? I would need help. I would need the Duke.

I smiled and again bowed.

"Well, I had best be on my way then; I need to be far away from here," I said.

"You still think he will lose!" the Duke exclaimed.

"No. he will win, but it doesn't matter. It will not be safe here," I said.

"But once the dragon is dead, all will be safe."

"Do you recall a certain peasant uprising in Marco?" I asked.

"Yes. Some serfs killed their lord Marco and declared themselves free," the Duke snorted.

"What happened?" I asked.

"The king called us to action. I sent a hundred men."

"And the peasants?"

"Hung from trees, drawn and quartered," the Duke said with a warm smile.

"An example was made."

"Of course," the Duke said. "What's this to do with Goodwin?"

"Not Goodwin, rather your realm and the realms around you. To the South is the Duchy of Rubabar. My guild-sister Olga Oakenboard negotiated a contract between Duke Rubabar and Bone-Melter seven years ago."

"Bone-Melter?" the Duke asked.

"The dragon that occupies Rubabar's lands," I said.

"What is it about these dragons and their names!" the Duke exclaimed.

"I know, I know," I said.

"Does it actually melt bones?"

"Frequently and with great relish," I replied.

"Why?"

"Something about the marrow..."

"Egads!" the Duke said. He looked at me with disgust, as if I were the one melting bones.

"Why are you bringing up Rubabar's dragon?" Nurble asked.

"For the same reason, I bring up your Eastern neighbor Baron Horegirth and his dragon, Skull-Spitter."

"Skull-Spitter?" the Duke said. "Does it actually spit out...?" the Duke pointed to his own head rather than finish the question.

"With great accuracy," I replied. "Can you guess what lies to the West?"

"I would hazard another dragon," he replied smartly.

"Two actually," I said, "a mated pair: Fire-Fart and its mate, Spiff the Sun Blocker."

"Well, I know there's no dragon to the North!" the Duke said as if this proved something.

"It's too cold; that is why a giant was there," I said.

"So that's why the Baron Bungbole never has to hire your lot. Seems unfair."

"Indeed, he is blessed," I said, not bothering to point out that the Baron could barely grow enough crops to feed himself or his people, let alone giants.

"Why are you telling me about all these other dragons? They are not my concern. Blood-Wind is the problem."

"They are not your concern now," I said. "But what happens when these other dragons learn that Blood-Wind's been killed? Just like you did with the peasants, they'll set an example. Can Sir Goodwin slay four dragons? They will fly here and destroy everything," I said.

The Duke's lower lip quivered a bit, but he swallowed hard. "Nonsense," he said, "you talk as if they were men; they are beasts."

"Beasts who can negotiate a contract, sign one with a tail dipped in ink, tally peasants delivered, read a manifest; beasts with long, long memories."

"You're trying to frighten me," the Duke said.

"You should be frightened," I said.

"Piffle! They are beasts; nothing will happen."

I sighed. It was clear the Duke would never come around. The idea of killing the dragon was too appealing. I made a quick calculation. I should be safe if I bought a horse and rode to the North immediately. It would be tight but manageable.

I did not move.

At first, I thought that my pride kept me there, or perhaps fear of the damage to my reputation. What else could it be? Why should I care about the people of Nurble? They didn't care about me. All I got from them were looks of suspicion, even hate. They called me 'Dragon-lover', 'ghoul', 'flesh-trader'.

But that didn't mean they deserved death. I've seen what happens when you rebel against a dragon: burned bodies and wrecked buildings, stones cracked and iron melted, ash stretching for miles, pools of poison and acid where once lay fields and ponds.

I looked at the Duke. He didn't know; he didn't understand dragons; he only understood his world, the world of nobles. Perhaps that was the answer...

"Fine," I said. "Let's speak of more practical matters. How was Sir Goodwin rewarded for slaying that giant?"

"Betrothed to the Bungbole's daughter," the Duke replied.

"Isn't there a rivalry between you and Bungbole, a dispute over farmland?"

"What of it?" the Duke asked.

"Why would the future son-in-law of your rival aid you?"

"He seeks glory," the Duke said.

"Indeed, after he slays the dragon, your peasants will cheer him. How do you feel about the next Baron of Bungbole being idolized by your subjects?" I asked.

Finally, the Duke looked afraid.

"You think Sir Goodwin plans to overthrow me?" he asked.

"Sir Goodwin is a genuinely noble soul, but his future father-in-law, the good Baron? You know him well. What kind of man is he?" I knew the answer: a treacherous bastard, just like Nurble.

The Duke sank into his chair. He resembled a deflated pig bladder.

"I am lost," he said.

I smiled.

"We must stop Goodwin," I said.

"How?" the Duke asked.

"Poison?" I asked.

The Duke's eye glanced toward the hidden bookshelf.

"Such an act would be ignoble," the Duke said softly.

"Agreed," I said. "And with that dragon blood in him, he might resist the poison. Besides, he is fasting. The only medium would be the holy wine he takes at mass."

"To poison sacramental wine would be a grave sin," the Duke said; his tone was more thoughtful than shocked.

"An unthinkable act," I replied. I looked down at the table, where the glove still rested.

I picked up the glove and waved it triumphantly.

"I have the answer," I said.

"What? The glove? Can we use it against Goodwin somehow?" the Duke asked. He snatched the glove from me and began examining it.

"You misunderstand. I can show the glove to the dragon. Explain the danger. If the dragon knows beforehand that the knight is fire-proof and preternaturally strong, it can fight him on its own terms. Fly up and drop boulders on him or something. True, Goodwin will die, but at least he'll die a hero's death, and my warning will allow me to ask for a further reduction in our offering."

"And you will reap even more gold," the Duke said, giving me a speculative look.

"I am willing to refund the addition to you," I said.

The Duke looked skeptical.

"A dragon negotiator willing to take a cut in commission? It's unheard of," the Duke said.

Like everyone, the Duke assumed I was only in it for the money. Never mind the burned bodies and wrecked towers that would come if we didn't stop the knight. No one ever understands until it's too late.

"Consider it a further incentive. I prefer to continue dealing with you rather than Baron Bungbole," I lied. "He's a Northern bumpkin; you are sophisticated. Besides, after this, I'll have such a good rapport with Blood-Wind that future dealings will be much easier, far more lucrative. I'm willing to set aside profit today for greater profit tomorrow." The Duke smiled at the explanation. With an overly formal gesture, as if he wore bestowing a medal, he handed the glove back to me.

"Go and keep an eye on the knight," I said. "Keep him occupied in prayer, and I will go to the dragon."

Duke Nurble sighed.

"Ah well, I suppose we have no choice. Such a shame," the Duke said, shaking his head.

"A ruler must make difficult choices," I said, "You must protect yourself and your kingdom above all else. It's for the greater good — for your subjects and heirs."

"Yes. I must think of my heirs," the Duke answered. Again, his tone was thoughtful, which should have alerted me. Sighing one last time, he heaved himself up and departed.

I waited, collecting my thoughts, formulating how I should approach the dragon. Then I made my way out of the library and towards the courtyard and the gate.

It was evening. The castle walls cast long shadows. In the shadows, I saw movement. Lank, helmeted figures were following me. I picked up my pace; my companions did also. Ahead, two came into view, crossing their halberds to make a barricade. Behind me, I heard movement. I spun and saw one of the Duke's guards lunging for me, a club in hand. I dodged one blow, but another guard came forward, then another. They raised their clubs. I tried to run, but they had me surrounded. The clubs came down. Darkness engulfed me.

I woke in a dungeon, my head aching. I was in chains, and I could hear the slow drip of water. The Duke stood before me.

"I take it you changed your mind," I said.

"You were most convincing, especially regarding how my vassals would view Sir Goodwin. That's really what persuaded me that you were on to something," he said.

"I am," I said. "It's not too late."

"It was what you said about him being a hero. You see, Sir Goodwin is already a hero in the Count's land. He has already slain a giant there. So I suggested to Sir Goodwin that he break his engagement to the Count's daughter and marry my daughter instead: she is prettier and her dowry larger. The good knight agreed. So now I, and not the Count, will have a hero as a son-in-law. A double hero once he kills the dragon."

"The other dragons will not stand for it," I warned.

"Tush, I doubt they will care, and if they do, then you can negotiate an agreement. You will stay here a few days so as not to interfere, and then I will release you."

I thought of arguing, but realized it was pointless. I looked around: the walls were damp, the air cold. I felt a glimmer of hope, not for the Duke or his realm but for myself.

"This is a deep dungeon," I said.

"Yes, we are far underground. Once, there was a tower above. I had it torn down for my chateau, but I kept the underpinnings. I knew this dungeon would be useful. Make no trouble, or this place will be your tomb."

Smiling, the Duke departed. I wondered how long he would be smiling. Carefully, I sat down. My head was still reeling from the clubs. I felt nauseous. Was it from my battered skull or my predicament, or both? I couldn't tell. My mind went round in circles. I had misjudged the Duke. I had underestimated the knight. I was bad at reading people. Perhaps it was due to all my time dealing with dragons. Maybe it was because so many people viewed me as being on par with dragons: another creature feeding off human sacrifice. It had hardened me. I had spent too much time drinking in taverns alone, celebrating my victories alone. Instead of sharing what I had done with others, convincing them that what I did was for the best (despite how ugly and monstrous it seemed), I'd wallowed in self-pity. And now I would pay the price. I would die down here, unless this dungeon really was as deep and damp as I hoped it was.

My guard was named Grugney. He was a dim-witted soul who thought nobles were on par with angels. Grugney told me that Sir Goodwin had triumphed. A great feast was taking place above, and the Duke, with tremendous largess, had sent down a plate of roasted dragon meat. Out of professional courtesy, I did not eat it. Grugney thought me a fool and ate it himself. I am not sure how much time passed, but after what seemed like days, I was awakened by the sound of rumbling. The ground shook. I heard distant screams. I knew that above me, a great fire raged. Fortunately, the air down here was clean. Smoke rises and I was underground.

Eventually, Grugney came to my cell. His face was covered in tear-stained soot.

"Dragons!" he cried. "The sky is full of dragons!"

"Perhaps the Duke should send Sir Goodwin out," I said.

"Goodwin is dead! They picked him up and dropped him from up high. Everything is on fire. You must come. You must stop them!"

I shook my head.

"There is no stopping them. Do you want to live, Grugney?"

"Yes! Save me!" Grugney cried. Finally, someone had said something sensible.

"Open the door," I said.

He did so.

"Unchain me," I said.

He did so.

"Are there stores down here? Water and food?" I asked.

"Yes."

"Then we will wait it out," I said.

Grugney stared at me in horror, but a look of resignation came to his face. He nodded in agreement and sat down on the floor in a hunch, hiding his face.

Over the next two days, we heard many screams, explosions, and roars. They must have been very loud to reach down here. It was rough on poor Grugney. He cowered in a corner of the cell, crying for much of the time.

I tried to shut the sound out. I spent as much time as I could recalling all the details I knew about the four dragons above. Skull-Spitter would be playfully spitting heads at various targets. Bone-Melter would be eating hot marrow, and Fire-Fart? Well, he had that name for a reason. As to his mate, she would probably be judiciously comparing her current paramour to the other two males. I recalled a report that Silas Strenk had written about Skull-Spitter. It noted Spitter as highly intelligent and judicious, even for a dragon. The report described him as copper in color. As for Bone-Melter, I had heard that he was scarred from fights with other dragons; he had a bad reputation in the guild. There was little information on the mated pair. Hopefully, all four would be gone when we emerged.

Eventually, there was silence.

Was it over?

We crawled up and out.

Ruin greeted us.

Grugney fell to his knees. The look on his face was a microcosm of horror. Tears streamed down his cheeks, and his mouth trembled: all his angels were dead. Then he fainted, which was probably for the best. If he was anything like me, he'd be over the worst of it when he woke. I had been about his age when my village had tried to rebel.

I scouted ahead; it was as I expected. The Duchy of Nurble was no more. The town, the farms, the Duke's castle were destroyed. Sir Goodwin's lance was sticking upright atop a pile of rubble like a pole. Stuck upon it, like a flag at half-mast, was Sir Goodwin. I suspect the dragons had dropped him multiple times from the sky. His armor stopped fire; falling was another matter. At the base of the lance was the Duke's body, burned to a crisp. He looked like a roasted pig.

All around, I heard moans and cries. It was difficult to tell where the sounds came from until one realized they were coming from everywhere. Above, the sun was obscured, the sky full of smoke. I stumbled forward, making my way to a tall, smoke-obscured tower that was somehow still standing. Then the tower moved.

A low, rumbling noise, like a huge Catherine wheel being turned on chains, echoed around me.

Wings emerged from the side of the 'tower', and I realized that the dragons had not left. An immense, fanged face, eyes shining with cunning and confidence, emerged from the smoke. To my left, I heard the padding of enormous feet; another head appeared, peering down at me with dispassionate contempt. To my right, two more heads, necks tenderly intertwined, growled both amorously and hungrily.

Like the Duke's lands, I was surrounded by dragons. The one ahead stared at me for a moment more, then began to open its mouth.

I nearly froze but willed myself to move; I bowed as best I could, flourishing my hands in supplication.

"It is an honor to meet you, oh illustrious Spitter of Skulls," I said, keeping my voice calm. Inwardly, I prayed that the report I had read on Skull-Spitter's coloration was accurate.

The dragon ahead, copper in color, paused in mid-breath, then cocked its head to one side.

"Guild?" it growled.

"Yes, I am Edwin of the Negotiators Guild at your service."

"I would think that a member of the guild would know better than to have allowed this," the dragon said. It *was* Skull-Spitter.

"Rest assured, I tried to prevent it. I was locked in the dungeon below this former keep by its owner." I pointed to the roasted pig. "The Duke would not listen to reason. He was going to have me executed for attempting to warn Blood-Wind."

"For that, your death will be swift," Skull-Spitter said.

I wanted to run. I wanted to scream. I even wanted to fight (how, I don't know), but I knew none of that would save me. I had to think and think quickly.

"Thank you," I said, bowing again. "I, of course, understand. It is a shame that the guild will not. They will view all of you with great distrust when they hear of this tragic incident. The circumstance will look most suspect. It appears you decided to carve up Blood-Wind's territory for yourselves."

"Nonsense," Skull-Spitter said.

"Of course," I replied quickly, "but consider how ludicrous it will seem that a knight slew a dragon. No one will believe that a man," I pointed to Sir Godwin's half-mast corpse, "slew the great Blood-Wind."

This gave Skull-Spitter pause.

"It's stalling," the one to my right said. "Kill it and be done with it."

"As a trusted guild member, I could write a report explaining what happened; it would only be circulated among the upper leadership. This could all be kept quiet — something we all want. No one wants more incidents like this."

To my left, Fire-Fart spoke. "Aren't you that Edwin who wrote that piece on Dragon Counting systems in the quarterly?"

"I am, oh great scaled one," I said.

"I quite liked that," the dragon said.

"I've always thought the draconic use of base eight rather than ten to be superior," I said.

"Of course. After all..."

"Eight is a power of two," I interjected hastily.

"Exactly," Fire-Fart said, nodding. Dragons love maths. They love gold and eating people more, but mathematics is a close third.

"You should do a study on egg combinatorics," Fire-Fart said speculatively.

"I am planning one, actually," I lied. "Should I survive."

Ahead of me, Skull-Spitter's head lowered and came close to me.

"Now, I remember you. You negotiated a contract for my niece a few years ago. She said you were quite good."

"Your niece is as nearly discerning as you, oh great spitter of heads." I bowed my own head as I spoke.

"She is clever," Skull-Spitter said proudly. Male dragons are often more fond of their nieces and nephews than their own (supposed) offspring. This is due no doubt to the overly amorous nature of female dragons, but I did not say this. *Never piss off the dragon.*

"Well, what do the rest of you think?" Skull-Spitter asked.

"Remember, my lord, you will need to negotiate this new territory between you, not to mention new contracts with the respective humans in your expanded territories. There will also need to be a master contract with the guild," I said. With each tedious item I listed, I could see the dragons almost wince. They hate such details.

"Oh, spare him. Fire-Fart will be mopey if he doesn't get that piece on egg maths," this came from Spiff, Fire-Fart's mate.

"Well, I want to melt his bones," Bone-Melter said, not surprisingly.

"You've been melting bones all day," Skull-Spitter said. "I'm with Sun Blocker. He'll be useful."

"I agree," Fire-Fart said.

"Very well," Bone-Melter growled. With a great leap, he flew into the sky. The gust nearly knocked me over.

"Remember to cover combinatorics of first-ordered egg pairs," Fire-Fart said.

"Farewell," Spiff said, more to Skull-Spitter than to me.

"Well, little human, you're quite clever for one of your kind," Spitter said.

I said nothing: compliments from dragons are not always a welcome thing. The dragon continued.

"You have your work cut out for you. Of course, you'll make quite a killing off this." A low chuckle came from Skull-Spitter's mouth. It was the first time I had ever heard a dragon laugh.

"The only ones killing here are you and your kind," I said hotly. It simply leapt out of me.

Skull-Spitter growled. I had violated the first rule. I had pissed off the dragon. Was I to die after all?

Instead, the dragon raised his head high and roared. I nearly shat myself from the sound. My head, still recovering from those mace blows, was instantly splitting.

"Even you don't understand," Spitter said. "You humans need us. You may hate us, but trust me, the world would be a real horror show without us dragons around to keep your kind in check. These warrens of yours would get bigger and bigger. Pretty soon, you'd be living like rats, and you'd ruin the land, breeding like crazy. You think this is bad?" Its swept one wing over the surrounding ruin. "This nothing to what the world would look like if your kind was in charge. No, you're far too dangerous to go unchecked. Without us, you'd become real monsters."

Then he laughed again, and with a great leap, he flew straight up and disappeared into the smoke. I knew he would be home soon, curled up and dreaming dragon dreams in his warren, which was undoubtedly called Death-Cap or Fear-Spike or some other ridiculous name.

I sat down on a pile of rocks and began to plan. There was a lot to do: reports to write, proposals to draft. I wanted to get started, but I stopped. I could hear the cries of the survivors. Someone would have to find the able-bodied, organize them, gather food and water, build shelters. The convent had probably been spared. I could get word to the nuns. It was work that would be profitless, maybe even thankless, but it would have to come first. After all, they were my people. Anything else was too monstrous to consider.

See Christopher Warden's story "The Dragon's Due" online at Metaphorosis.
If you liked it, leave a comment. Authors love that!
Remember to subscribe to our e-mail updates so you'll know when new stories are posted.

About the story

Beyond an ever-present desire to turn things upside down, this story was inspired by the "Fable of the Dragon Tyrant" metaphor tale made popular by

Oxford philosopher Nick Bostrom and the you-tuber personality CGP Grey. The argument was that we should try and get rid of aging; it was presented as a fable about people paying tribute to a dragon. I found the whole thing naive, misguided, and, frankly, destructive. It actually made me angry. I think this story is my act of rebellion against the notion of fighting against things that we should be wise enough to accept. It's not always reasonable or even safe to tilt at windmills; sometimes, the results can be disastrous.

That initial impulse then grew as I thought about the notion of "heroes" and crusaders: both the big macho type and the righteous do-gooders who have no self-doubt and can't be made to question their purpose. I liked the idea of a narrator who wasn't charismatic or well-liked but who was cursed with being right.

A question for the author

Q: What's a genre you'd like to write, but don't or can't?

A: I would love to write a heist story. I think this goes back to my childhood dream of being a cat burglar. Nailing down all the details has discouraged me from pursuing it.

About the author

Chris Warden is a native of California. He is married to Jane Warden; they have two adult children. Chris graduated from U.C. Berkeley with a degree in philosophy. He has worked as a web developer, computer programmer, game designer, and UX developer.

He enjoys body surfing, body boarding, and ocean swimming. He spends an inordinate amount of time in the ocean but has still not figured out how to breathe underwater.

www.criswar.com/write

Through the Middle

J.B. Kish

There's a woman driving slowly down highway 27 in their direction, and every couple of miles, she opens her window and lets a handful of something human-tasting scatter in the wind. Ashes, Rory suspects. She misses the man who's now dust and cries a little as she goes, singing Bill Withers because the radio doesn't play much more than static and gospel out this far. Bump thinks the powdered man must have liked Bill Withers very much.

At the speed she's going, she'll reach the diner in about thirty minutes. Rory presses a finger into the countertop and

thanks Bump for the heads up. Then he
puts on a fresh pot of coffee. Coffee's a
good start for sadness like this, Rory
thinks, and he should know. He's only
just found happiness again.

Rory sits behind the counter, shaped
like a farm egg. He's put on weight that
rounds him. Muscular legs stick out
beneath his body like a pair of clearance
sale limbs not intended for him, and he
wears the rest of his skin like thick diving
dress, rich with small folds that retreat
from his ribs and neck. His body is a
game of hide and seek: American
traditional appearing around each corner.
There's a woman in a bathing suit diving
down his forearm. A faded anchor on his
bicep. Twin sparrows on his chest that no
longer fly straight.

Half an hour passes, and her Civic
pulls up to the far-flung roadside diner.
Rory plays "Grandma's Hands" on the
jukebox and pours a fresh cup of coffee.
The woman walks in with a newborn
puppy, and he greets her warmly. When
she hears Bill Withers, she buckles a
little, and Rory helps her to a nearby
booth. "Here," he says, placing a ceramic
mug in front of her. "This will make you
feel better."

Rory disappears into the kitchen and fixes the woman—her name is Aliyah—something to eat. For a long time, Aliyah reclines in the booth and stares at the sunset with the puppy in her lap. Her t-shirt is cotton-white, floating elegantly above a pair of cut off shorts and some skateboard sneakers. The skin of her cheek is pocked with dark acne scars that she's not covered up. She looks like the subject in a Rockwell painting.

Bump asks who Rockwell is and Rory places a finger on the wall like he's using a walkie talkie. Silently, he explains Norman Rockwell was an artist who used to paint restaurants like theirs. Then Rory slides a turkey sandwich in front of Aliyah and asks if she'd appreciate company. She accepts politely, and he wonders for one terrifying moment what he—an old man in his seventies—can offer this woman, if anything. He knows nothing about being young or black or growing up in these times. But he has an ear, which is all she seems to need, and Aliyah explains she's wandering southern Oregon, spreading her father's ashes. He was one of the west coast's most celebrated archeologists, and he died peacefully of old age a month ago. After an hour, Aliyah makes an embarrassed face. She's been talking this whole time and hasn't asked Rory one question about himself.

Rory prefers it this way. He doesn't like talking about his father or the Navy; he's not the kind of discarded thing that complains. Anyway, nothing before matters because this is where he matters most. Of course, Aliyah doesn't understand that at all and surprises him by asking, *What's next.*

Rory laughs through his nose. "The only way this diner shuts down is because I've died and there's no one left to open it."

"Suppose you win the lottery."

He sips his coffee too quickly and wets his mustache; Aliyah grins as he dabs his mouth dry. "I grew this thing in the Navy because I had a baby face. My commanding officer said it would make me look smart."

"Did it?"

Rory nods and sits back. "In the Navy, you know exactly where you matter most. They tell you where to be and what to do. How to shave, how to dress. After I got out, I spent a long time searching for value again. When I found this restaurant and its customers, I *did* win the lottery. I don't think I could ever walk away from that."

Aliyah ponders his words a while before dismissing them with the wave of a hand; he can't help but fall in love with her a little. *Aliyah's* value, she explains, chases her like the puppy on her lap. She gets job offers because her father had important friends and they think her trowel was destined to continue his legacy. But she doesn't want a life in the dirt. She wants to start a vegan bakery. "But is that a terrible idea?"

It's not, and Rory envies how clearly she sees herself.

"You know, I've heard of you," Aliyah says. He points to his breast, and she nods. "They say there's a hermit in the desert that helps people. That's you, I think."

He shrugs. "Most folks know what they need. Sometimes they have to hear it a specific way."

On the way out the door, she thanks him for good company and happy coincidences. "Bill Withers was my father's favorite, you know."

Rory holds up a finger and fetches a cup of coffee to-go. "For the road," he explains, and then he grabs a handful of sugar packets from the table. "And for the bakery."

Aliyah chuckles at the gift and gives Rory a squeezing hug. "We'll see."

His heart beats like a young man's as she heads down the road. It was a nice cup of shared coffee, he thinks. Coffee's always a good start for sadness like that. Then Bump asks if Norman Rockwell can come paint their restaurant, and Rory laughs before turning in for the night.

Bump came through the middle.

That's the only way he's able to tell it. One day, he 'passed through the middle and surfaced here', just about the same as most customers. He could be extraterrestrial, but Bump didn't come from the great above. He came from deep, deep below, 'through the middle', and burst up against the ground like a pimple on the cheek of southern Oregon's desert.

Rory never tries to dig him up because it wouldn't be polite, and Bump seems satisfied enough to exist under the asphalt bloom behind the diner, which houses him like a geodesic dome. Besides, Bump says the asphalt is what connects him to the road and the people traveling their way. It's through this that he can feel the vibration of human emotions, touch palms through cracked leather steering wheels, and read Rory the prologue of their customers. It's what makes the pair a uniquely wonderful team, and why Rory is truly happy for the first time in a long while.

This is why Rory's stomach drops when Bump says someone is coming, but he can't sense anything about them. Bump can perceive the subtle weight of their body through the driver's side tires, but the rest feels eerie and quiet. It's almost as if there's no one there at all. *Can Mustangs drive themselves on this planet?* he asks Rory realizes he's not breathing and tries to inhale casually.

Anyway, says Bump. *They should be here tomorrow afternoon.*

But first, there's a man and a woman—a college couple in their twenties—coming down the highway, and whenever she brings up his temper, he wrings the steering wheel in a way she can't see. His little outbursts are growing more frequent, and even though he apologizes, they seem to be dancing around an incident— something like a *push* or maybe a *fall*, Bump says. They can't agree on which. The woman is assertive, but occasionally her voice is nervous around the edge. Rory thanks Bump for the heads up. With a frown, he puts on a fresh pot of coffee. Coffee's a good start when dealing with men like this. As it drips, he can't help his mind wandering to his tools out back and finds himself asking how hard it might be to dig a man-sized hole.

You'll not stick him down here with me, Bump jokes.

A while later, the bell rings, and without asking, Rory pours two fresh cups of coffee.

A tattooed woman appears at his counter, looks down with a smile, and dubs him a saint. She holds the ceramic mug under her nose with both hands and breathes deep. She's brunette and diamond shaped, with as much life as a fresh battery. When the boyfriend appears over her shoulder, he has a square head and practiced neutrality. A chameleon: Rory spots it right away. Polite. Jovial. Makes pleasant conversation all the way up until he leaves for the bathroom, which is outside around back. Rory forgets to mention the very specific jimmy required to unlock its door from inside, and that buys him a while to chat.

He places a pastrami sandwich in front of the tattooed woman with a roll of silverware. Her jaw drops playfully, and she asks why Rory owns a diner in the absolute middle of nowhere.

"Pills," he says candidly because she needs to hear this a specific way. She doesn't follow. "When I got out of the Navy, I took a job as a line cook and spent thirty years making people happy. And then we got bought out; I was fired by a hot shot celebrity for not understanding molecular gastronomy. No one in Portland wants to hire an old cook with bad knees, so when I hit the bottom, I drove down here to eat enough Oxycodone to put me in the ground."

Her eyes grow wide, and she has the packed cheek of a squirrel.

Rory smiles, easing a bit of this uninvited tension, "I found this restaurant instead."

The woman smiles uncomfortably. "Good for you." She tries to end the conversation on a high note. "So many five-star ratings online, you must be doing something right."

Suddenly Bump is there, in Rory's mind. *The mustang is going much faster. It will be here sooner,* he says.

Rory's heart skips a beat. What *is* all this nonsense about self-driving cars and phantom drivers? He discretely presses his right fingertip into the counter. The entire finger has vibrated with heat since the day he met Bump, when he pressed down on the asphalt dome curiously, and their connection was calcified. He theorizes it's a kind of foreign energy that comes from the other side—through the middle. When he presses down, he can sense its vein-like release, connecting him from the counter to the floor below, which joins with the building's foundation, the earth around, and ultimately allows him to project thoughts to his friend out back. *You're imagining things,* he tells Bump, and then he lifts his finger, ending the conversation.

Rory returns to the woman, distracted. "The point is," he continues, "it wasn't good enough to keep telling my family I'd change. People tell themselves they can just wake up tomorrow and *do better*. But I had to work at it. Leave an unhealthy environment, change my life. Otherwise, all those good intentions were just smoke and vapor."

The woman's eyes narrow slightly.

He makes a noise in the back of his throat, then nods toward the bathroom. "What I'm saying is, people don't magically wake up and *do better*. Unless he does the work, his apologies are just smoke and vapor." Then Rory tops off her coffee. "Understand?"

The blood drains from the woman's face and the bell rings over her shoulder. "Old man," her boyfriend growls. He walks up to the counter and throws the key into Rory's chest. It lands against the floor with a jingle. "Bathroom door is broken as hell." Then he nudges the woman with his elbow. "Hurry up and pay."

The whole interaction was a bit heavier handed than Rory prefers. When they've left, he walks out to the road and stares into the distance. He envisions a Mustang blowing fire from its tailpipe, riding a cloud of smog. And then, for reasons he cannot explain, he thinks of constructing a white tower for the first time in years.

What would you do if I passed back through the middle? Bump asks.

The sun is tangerine-orange and quickly fading. Rory flips a chicken breast on the charcoal grill he's rolled out back. With an elderly groan, he touches a finger to the ground. *You know it's rather unfair that I must speak through my finger, but* you *can project your thoughts directly into me.*

Humans are surprisingly complex, Bump answers. *Would you stay at the diner?*

Rory is annoyed and tense. *I'd climb the white tower and throw myself off,* he snips.

Bump is quiet a while, then says, *The mustang will be here soon.*

"Lord!" Rory shouts with his actual voice. "What is all this about?"

When Bump doesn't respond, Rory splays his fingers in frustration. "Fine," he says, "Let it come," and he walks inside. He grabs a large piece of parchment paper and writes 'PERMANENTLY CLOSED', then tapes it to the front door and kills the lights. There's not a single glowing bulb in the entire dining room. Out back, he waves a dismissive hand at bump and takes his dinner to bed.

He's here, Bump whispers.

Rory opens his eyes with a start, then sticks his head out the trailer door and spots a light in the restaurant. "He?"

The one driving the Mustang. He's waiting for you inside.

"It's nearly five in the morning."

You should go in, is all Bump says.

Inside, there's a handsome man sitting at the counter eating a bag of potato chips. He looks like he stepped off a Hollywood movie set, but Rory can't decide why. His features are elusive: Latin American one moment, Eastern European the next. There is a fresh pot of coffee on the counter, and he invites Rory to join him.

"Who are you?" Rory whispers, looking down at his parchment paper sign, which has been folded into a perfect square on the counter.

"Name's *Very Hungry*," the man says with a punchline smile. It's a joke, but Rory's not laughing. The stranger reaches into his pocket and pulls out three one-hundred-dollar bills. "Can you make the perfect burger?"

Well now, just what in the hell is this? Rory wonders. *And why are you suddenly so damned quiet?* he asks Bump through the countertop. Bump doesn't answer.

"Every time I come here, I can't wait to get my hands on a real American cheeseburger." The stranger makes two fists. "But you can't go to a drive thru. What's the point of anticipation if the food's no good?" He slides the money forward. "Three hundred dollars for the best burger you can make."

Rory scowls. Breaking into his diner—scaring his friend—that's one thing. Questioning his ability on the grill is another entirely! He takes the money and draws up his torso. "I'll make it to-go."

Rory returns with possibly the greatest hamburger he's ever made. Carefully sculpted. Cooked to perfection. Golden French fries that could usher in the seventh trumpet! Lettuce so crisp it looked plastic!

And what does he find waiting for him? Nothing.

The Mustang is still parked outside, but there's no one sitting behind the counter.

Rory, says Bump.

He closes his eyes. *Shit*, he thinks, keeping this particular thought to himself. Cautiously, he walks out back and finds the handsome man standing above Bump, looking down at the asphalt dome with a mouth full of potato chips. Rory licks his lips and presses a finger into a wooden railing. "What is this?" he asks.

Rory, says Bump, *this is Hadrian. Hadrian, this is Rory.*

Hadrian waves and smiles. It's not unkind, and Rory hates him for that.

Hadrian is my grandchild, adds Bump.

Inside, the to-go box is empty. Rory is three hundred dollars richer, and he's never felt worse.

Hadrian is here to take Bump home. Bump left without telling anyone, and at his age, he really needs to be looked after. A depression drapes over Rory like a series of blankets, one after the other. He feels heavier the longer Hadrian talks.

"But," Rory whispers. "We're quite good friends."

"That's a funny pair," suggests Hadrian. The sun illuminates the diner with a warm glow. Dust floats along the rays of light like sad poetry.

"I've come to care for your grandfather very deeply," explains Rory. He finds himself appealing to the man's sense of empathy, but who's to say if Hadrian has any to begin with. His kind comes through the middle and takes on a form that emulates the planet's inhabitants. That didn't necessarily mean they possess the same emotional capacity. "Perhaps he could stay here with me?" Rory's smile is desperate.

Hadrian shakes his head. "Grandfather got stuck trying to emerge. It happens occasionally. I'm here to help." He takes a long sip of coffee and sighs gratefully. "Have you considered what you'll do when Bump passes back through the middle?"

Rory's too scared of the white tower to answer, so Hadrian adds, "Would you like to pass through the middle with us instead?"

Through the middle—it's a terrifying notion! Timid, he whispers, "Your grandfather's never told me much about where you come from. And this is my home."

"So, you wish to stay here?"

"I wish for things to stay as they are!"

"They cannot," Hadrian says in a way that's not unkind. "We leave tonight."

Tears gallop down Rory's cheek. It's just like life to do this to him again. The bell over the door rings, and Rory jumps. Quickly, he dries his cheeks and waves hello to a pair of men with a young boy. Farmers perhaps? "Be right with you," he calls. "Grab a seat anywhere."

Rory plucks his apron from the counter, pausing long enough to ask Bump why he didn't give a heads up on their new customers.

"I've suspended your connection to my grandfather," Hadrian whispers. "Only temporarily."

Suspended their connect—how dare he! What kind of game was he playing? Rory's face is beet read. He opens his mouth to shout when—

"Hey fella," one of the men calls. "Coffees and a juice."

Rory is shaking. Gradually, his expression lifts upward and he fetches their order. Standing above them, he withdraws a pad of paper and a pencil, clears his throat, and wonders why he's so uneasy.

"Y'all from around here?"

Neither man looks up from their menus. They're vaguely like one another. Brother's maybe? Or perhaps it's just coincidence. The youngest, a boy of ten or eleven, stares out the window thoughtfully. He has a book on his lap—*The Spectator Bird*—but never opens it. The eldest, a leathery man with ruddy cheeks, looks down at his wristwatch and speaks in a way that's not intended for Rory. "Two hours," he whispers.

The other nods and looks up from his menu. "Three omelets, bacon, white toast all around."

Rory notes the order and retrieves the menus. "Beautiful day out there."

The younger man slides his cup forward. "Top off, please."

As Rory steps back into the kitchen, Hadrian raises a polite finger. "I'd love one of those omelets, if it's not a complete bother."

The kitchen door swings shut, and for a long while, Rory stares at the range. Slowly, he begins making the order. It's easy. It's muscle memory. He could make omelets in his sleep, and without meaning it, his mind drifts to the white tower. He makes sure his index finger isn't touching anything that connects him to Bump, and he's ashamed of it. *How much is left?* he wonders. He is pulled from the question by the distinct smell of eggs starting to burn. He saves the omelets just in time. Again, it's muscle memory. He really could do this in his sleep.

After breakfast, the man with ruddy cheeks pays and Rory asks how everything was. "Sure," the man answers. "Good enough."

The blood drains from Rory's face as their truck pulls out the lot and disappears down the road. Hadrian picks at the men's leftovers while Rory dumbly removes his apron and floats outside, into his trailer, and opens the closet door. He pushes aside a few shirts and finds a shoebox tucked all the way in the back. Inside is an orange prescription bottle with ten tablets that make a maraca sound when he shakes them. His heart pounds as if it means to crack his ribs, and suddenly Rory can't breathe. He races outside for air.

Hadrian sits on a folding chair next to Bump, finishing a side of potatoes. After Rory's caught his breath, he drags a chair next to them and squeezes the plastic bottle between both hands.

Were you able to serve those men?
Bump asks.

Hadrian nods; he's allowed them to speak again.

"I was able to feed them," Rory answers. "If that's what you mean."

Quietly, he opens the plastic bottle and slides half the contents into his palm. They're heavier than he remembers, like they have somewhere important to be. He imagines them pecking through his skin and dropping out the back of his hand, so he stacks them one by one on his armrest before they can get away. Carefully, he constructs a beautiful white tower and envisions himself standing atop it, leaning out over a smooth, granite edge. The vast Oregon desert yawns beneath him, and his heart flutters at the brush of an old friend. An adrenaline he hasn't felt in years.

Rory's only closed his eyes for a moment when his chair nudges strangely, and when he looks back down, the tower is missing, and Hadrian is making a childish face. "These aren't good at all."

"You ate that?" Rory sits up as Hadrian dry swallows a white paste.

Hadrian's eyes widen. "The mints?"

"You can't have."

"Hadrian," Bump says. "Those were Rory's mints."

Rory presses a finger into his armrest. "They're not mints." Then to Hadrian, "You need to vomit."

"You mean on command?"

"Quickly."

"What happens if I don't?"

Rory doesn't answer, which is answer enough. "Oh." says Hadrian, sitting back. "Interesting."

"How exactly?"

"Well, if I don't, then my grandfather stays here, and you get what you want."

Rory's blood thickens with pressure. "I don't want your grandfather to be stuck here."

"But you don't want him to leave either"

"I don't want things to change." He's about to stand and force Hadrian to vomit himself. "What about our customers?"

"Will they stop coming?"

"How do you propose I help them without your grandfather here? Look what happened in there."

Hadrian makes a face like he finally understands the riddle in front of him. "My grandfather gives you value."

Rory draws himself upright. "Of course not."

"Is there someone else who does that?"

"His commanding officer," Bump says brightly.

Rory twists his hands anxiously. "My what?"

"You told the dust-man's daughter that your commanding officer made you grow that mustache and now you're smarter. He has given you value."

"No."

"You're not smart?"

"I was always smart."

"The mustache doesn't make you smart?"

"You need to throw up right now."

Hadrian holds out both palms like he didn't read that part of the human manual. "Do I punch myself?"

"Who then?" Bump asks.

"No one *gives* me value," Rory barks. "Stick your finger all the way down your throat until something happens."

Hadrian does as he's told.

Rory twist the cap onto the prescription bottle and stuffs the remaining pills into his pocket. "What would you have me do?" he growls. "Leave the diner tonight? Abandon my customers?"

"The diner gives you value," Bump clarifies.

"No." Rory pinches his brow and then points at Hadrian. "*Deeper.*" Hadrian grunts in acknowledgment and his finger descends another inch.

"Then what?"

"*I* do," Rory shouts. "I'm good at this. I'm good at helping people!" He stands and grabs Hadrian's elbow. He pushes upward and the man's finger disappears another inch. Hadrian gags fantastically; he vomits white bile onto Rory's clothes. It's unclear if he's disposed of all five pills, but Rory suspects it's enough. He's about to stumble backward when a small voice clears its throat: "Sir?"

They turn in surprise. The boy from breakfast peeks around the corner with a cautious expression. Rory let's go of Hadrian, who wipes his mouth and waves.

Bravely, the child asks, "You seen my book?"

"Book?" Then Rory understands. He waves the boy inside and searches the booth where they ate. He gets down on his hands and knees, hoping to find it under the table.

"What were you two fighting about?" the boy asks from behind.

"If I told you my mustache," Rory mutters, "would you believe me?"

Rory cranes his neck and spots the book wedged between the wall and booth. He reaches out and can nearly touch it with the tip of his finger, but Bump is idling there. Instead, Rory uses his ring finger to paddle at the book's spine until it falls to the floor.

Grunting, he shuffles backward and feels every vertebrae of his back unfurl. "Here." The boy takes the book and nods in thanks.

"Those men." Rory motions to the truck outside.

"My uncles."

"They don't talk much, do they?"

"Sure they do."

Sure they do. Rory's about to ask what terrible things they've been saying about breakfast when the boy turns and heads for the door.

"Wait—" Rory calls out and the child stops to look over his shoulder. Rory wants to ask; he's desperate to know, but a thick feeling of shame coats his throat. Frankly, the words are so dull in shape that even his mouth is bored with them, on top of which he's just realized how badly he stinks. The truth is, he's so insecure that this entire moment feels perfectly normal, and he hates himself for that.

The boy startles him by going first. "It doesn't matter if he doesn't like it."

Rory stops. He doesn't understand.

"Your mustache." The boy draws himself upward and walks across the checkered floor with raw, adolescent confidence. He places a companionable hand on Rory's bicep and says firmly, "I think it only matters if *you* like the mustache."

There's an inaudible *crack* of ivory-white granite.

With a radiant clap on his arm, the boy turns and jogs out. Rory opens and closes his mouth like a fish. His eyes have gently doubled in size, and there's a tangible warmth in his bicep. He floats to the window, and as the boy climbs up into the truck, he spots Rory. The boy waves and then reaches backward, withdrawing a plastic comb from his pocket. He holds it horizontally beneath his nose and smiles through the prongs.

Nothing here is as she remembers it. Aliyah sits in her Civic, staring up at the diner which is no longer the diner. It's *Dot's*, and Dot is a woman who doesn't allow dogs in her restaurant, so Koda waits in the car. Aliyah sits at a booth craning her neck, waiting for the hermit to round a corner.

Dot is a short Thai woman in her fifties who can carry more plates than seems possible. She tends to a busy dining room before dropping a cup of coffee in front of Aliyah. "Morning. Need some time or are you ready?"

"The man who worked here, an older gentleman."

Dot doesn't follow.

"He was the owner just a few months ago. Did he..." Aliyah tilts her head morbidly.

Dot shakes her chin no. "He sold."

Aliyah's stomach pirouettes. "He what?"

Dot smiles politely while scanning the restaurant from the corner of her eye. "If you need a little time with the menu..."

Aliyah nods and falls back into the booth, struggling to understand. She's driven all this way so he could talk her out of it. What's she supposed to do now?

Take the job and play secretary for a department of PhDs obsessed with her last name? How could this have happened?

The hermit *sold* his lottery?

Aliyah sips her coffee and stares at a caddy of sugar packets and room temperature creamer. Dot returns a while later and refills her cup.

"Did he say anything?" Aliyah asks. "Or where he was going?"

"Were you friends?" When Aliyah doesn't answer, Dot nods. "He sold quickly."

Aliyah knits her brow and chews the inside of her cheek. She can feel herself sinking inward.

"He left something." Dot speaks softly as if telling a secret. "A funny note taped out front with a couple urns of coffee." Then she turns and points to a bulletin board near the door. "I couldn't bring myself to throw it away."

When she spots the note, Aliyah's skin prickles. She climbs out of the booth and walks to the board.

Passed through the middle, she reads. *Help yourself to some coffee. No matter the problem, I've always found coffee is a good start.*

"Hon?" Dot's voice appears over her shoulder. "Do you need more time with the menu?"

Rubbing her thumb over the note, Aliyah shakes her head. She pays for a coffee to-go and Dot fetches her a paper cup. As she turns to leave, Aliyah plucks a few sugar packets from a nearby caddy. She pictures the old hermit in the desert who used to help people. Who told people things they knew, just said a specific way. Without thinking, she grabs a handful more. She stuffs her jacket pockets with little white packets until they are full. Pretty soon, she's emptying another caddy over a table and scooping them into her saddle bag.

"Hey!" Dot shouts from the register, her eyes wide.

Aliyah smiles apologetically as she empties a third caddy directly into her bag. Then a fourth.

"I said stop!" calls Dot, but the bell above the door is already ringing. Aliyah is racing to her car, shouting an apology through the window. She's got to get going!

Bill Withers glides into place as she and Koda soar down the highway toward home. Aliyah's turning down the job; she was never meant for a life in the dirt. She's decided to take her sugar packets and build something brand new.

See J.B. Kish's story "Through the Middle" online at Metaphorosis.
If you liked it, leave a comment. Authors love that!
Remember to subscribe to our e-mail updates so you'll know when new stories are posted.

About the story

A few years ago, I drove past a restaurant and found myself jotting down the concept for a new story: Guy pays $300 for the best hamburger someone can make. It didn't mean much to me at the time. I actually had no idea why someone would pay so much for a hamburger of all things. But I liked the imagery, and even though the idea would spend years collecting dust in my notes folder, it stuck with me.

This is how most of my stories come together. I capture small vignettes like that until I begin to see connective tissue. In the case of Through the Middle, the three notes that acted as the story's foundation were:

- Guy pays $300 for the best hamburger someone can make

- Diner in the middle of nowhere

- What if aliens didn't come from above, what if they came from below

I spent days mashing these ideas together, writing various outlines for how they might work. Sometimes the ideas just won't gel, no matter how hard I try. But "Through the Middle" was one of those wonderful, rare occasions where the story quickly began to tell itself.

A question for the author

Q: Do you have a garden? Have you ever grown your own food?

A: My wife is a hobbit of a woman. She spends most of her free time in our garden. While I've dabbled with a vegetable or two, she's got the green thumb in our family. During the summer, we spend a lot of time outside. I'm usually focused on a woodworking project while she's digging around in the dirt somewhere.

About the author

Originally from the Southwest, J.B. Kish moved to Portland, Oregon, in 2012. He is currently working on his second novel.

www.jbkish.com, @JohnBoyKish

Love, Death, and the Electric Soul

Alexandra Peel

"HushCabs. What's your location?"

"9 Trinity Heights. Quick as you can!"

"On our way, sir. Serina, you got this one?" The operator, Boyd, made it sound like a confirmation, rather than an ask.

Serina pulled a microfilament from her forearm port. The minute tube retreated into the Memory Loop device. The words, *'Of c-c-course I'm real, honey'*, settled on top of the pile of memories. The ML was playing up, again. She pocketed the gadget, irritated.

"I was just about to sign off." Serina sighed. Popped her neck left then right. Checked the holowatch on the dash. She'd been on since half six this morning. Ten hours, fifteen minutes.

"Tel and Brandy are mid-run. Kal's got a flyer. Trace and Pete called in sick. You're all I got."

She rolled her eyes at the two-way radio, "Aw shit. Got no one waiting for me, so may as well."

Brief pause. Faint hum before the radio crackled with Boyd's voice. Curt, though concerned. *"Don't go there, Serina. Just keep your shit together and grab the punter."*

She eased the cab out into traffic. Silent. The air-con wafted 'pine-scented' breeze across her face and exposed collar bones. She didn't have a clue what pine was. Something from the old times. Flowers, maybe? Checked the mirror, and glimpsed blue eyes underlined in blue shadows.

It took less than five minutes to skilfully navigate the early evening traffic; ducking between Old Hall, Roberts, and Paisley streets. She tapped a control. The driver's seat sighed as it expanded just enough to relieve the pressure on her backside and thighs. HushCabs could afford top tech, because they were exclusive, and charged more than most companies in the city. HushCabs weren't just quiet vehicles, they specialised in taking fares to places they didn't want colleagues, friends, or family to find out about. For whatever reason. It wasn't the company's business. They never asked. She had the door open as soon as she pulled into the pick-up zone. The customer easy to spot, practically dancing from one foot to the other in anticipation. Before he was even in, he blurted,

"Festival Gardens!" Just under six kilometres. Fifteen, maybe twenty minutes on clear roads. "You took your time. Hurry!" Serina glanced at the dash holowatch. It had taken her three minutes. She didn't argue. Never did. "I'll give you extra if you floor it!" his voice panicky.

She chuckled, "This isn't a movie, sir. We don't 'floor it'. There's lights, and crossings, not to mention a speed limit."

"Double!" he squeaked. Tempting, was the instant notion. But she didn't want to get pulled over and lose her license. Good jobs were not easy to come by these days.

Wow, this guy was seriously rattled. She watched him in her rear-view mirror. Not sitting back, sitting forward. Gripping the headrest of the front passenger seat with one hand. Glancing out the window, at his watch, her dash watch, and something in his other hand.

"I gotta get it back in time."

"Hmm hmm."

"Never been late before. Forgot the time. This once." She saw he had tears on his face. Started to feel uncomfortable. "God, I miss her so much when she's in there," he looked down at whatever was in his palm. "I love you, Laura honey."

She tried to concentrate on driving. Tried to block out her passenger's personal pain. Put her foot down on Sefton and Riverside. No lights along here. Back in the twenty-first century, the Advisory Council had turned off everything outside the prime cities. Save energy. Stop pollution. All that. Long after the space-based solar relays and Oceanic Energy Grid were operational, suburbs and abandoned industrial sites weren't fully reconnected — especially in towns and cities in the north. Halfway along Riverside, he gave her further directions. Past the old festival grounds — Pete had told her that there used to be actual gardens here. With trees. She supposed it must be true, otherwise, why would it have that name? Through some disused industrial site, finally coming to a halt outside a single isolated building.

"Want me to wait?" she asked as he dashed from the vehicle. Thought she caught a 'yeah'.

She plugged a microfilament from the dash into her forearm port. A syrupy voice inside her head — *Virtual cigarettes — for that healthier life choice.* She inhaled; habitual behaviour in response to pseudo stimulus, and looked at the place her ride had dashed into. Weeds occupied cracks in the paving. Single-storey building. Looked like a cross between a retro-style diner and a bunch of shipping containers. Polished chrome, once — hints glinting between rust and painted and cracked facade. Above the door, she could just make out part of a faded sign — Museum. She lowered the driver's window. A museum? Out here? Museum of what? Warm air hurried into the cool interior. The smell of dust. A hint of the not-too-distant river. If loneliness had an odour, this was it. She removed the dash port jack, pulled the small, black box from her pants pocket, and transferred to her Memory Loop. *'Just ch-ch-checking you're still real.'* *'Of course, I'm real, ho-neeeee—'* the voices stretched into distorted bass.

Her ride came walking out just then. Relieved. Like someone who had visited the bathroom. She whipped the jack out.

"Everything okay?" she asked as he settled back onto the rear seat. He nodded. His face was dry now. Looked like he'd washed it. "Back to Trinity Heights?" She started the cab.

"A drink. Anywhere. Any bar," he said.

He was silent the whole trip back. It took longer, the traffic heavier as more workers left at the end of their daily shifts. She pulled up outside The Furnace, a place she frequented, assuming he would want somewhere quiet.

"Join me." His request surprised her. "Come on, you must take a break some time."

You never fraternised with customers. You didn't want that sort of relationship, where they later used your 'friendship' as a bargaining tool for fare reductions. Plus, it was just weird. She shook her head. She'd go home. Alone. Jack in. Lie awake all night. Remembering.

"Listen," he said. "I got an eye for people. Y'know, facial tics, body language. Pardon me if I'm prying, but you look like someone who could do with a drink yourself. I sure as hell do. Drinking alone is crap. I promise I won't ask you to reduce my fare."

He must have read her mind, she thought. Her eyes went to the holowatch. Six-ten. Been on shift eleven hours, forty minutes. Fuck it. She parked the cab around the corner in an overnight bay. Followed him into the bar. Low-hanging light over each table. Gave the place an intimate feel despite its size. They took a two-seater next to the window. Ordered drinks. Sat in silence until the waiter returned.

"Cheers," he raised his glass and swallowed half before she had sipped hers. He let out a satisfied sigh. "Needed that."

For two hours, she and Frake; *first name Albert, don't like it, call me Frake,* consumed two bottles of house wine along with a selection of ales and liquors. As though each was trying to outdo the other. Very few words had been exchanged. But now, she stared at his blurred face as he said,

"I was returning my wife."

She thought she had misheard. Didn't respond. Frake took it as a sign to continue. Words slurring, hiccoughing intermittently, wiping tears. He was a PR man. Widowed. Told her the museum was a front for something else. It was a secret place where souls were stored. She spurted ale when she laughed. If she hadn't had a cavernous evening of sleeplessness before her, and if he'd been dressed like one of those Neo Dropout freaks, she'd have left. Souls! What a load of bollocks. We live, we die, and that's the end of it.

"Seriously." Hurt expression. "It's real," insistent. "They keep the souls of the dead. You can rent them out for a limited time. I heard about it from a colleague whose kid had died. Be with them again. Feel their company." He glanced up warily, "Talk to them." He spoke of Laura's smile. Laura's laughter. The way her nose wrinkled across the bridge when she giggled. She'd been killed in a hit and run. Sudden. Shocking. So young.

"Bull. Shit." He was having a joke at her expense. But he promised it was true. Outside the bar, he repeated something he'd said earlier.

"I can tell, y'know. When you've lost someone, you learn to see it in other people's faces. You lost someone too. Didn't you?"

She dismissed him. Angry. Caught the loop-train home. Lay on the rumpled bed. Plugged in her microfilament.

'Just ch-checking you're still real,' her own recorded voice said.

'Of course, I'm real, honey.'

Imagined the touch of his fingers on her cheek. She closed her eyes. He smiled and leaned in to kiss her. No contact. Loops were made from collected recordings, simulations, and holopics. You couldn't replicate physicality. His image flickered. This generally indicated a display driver issue. Or prolonged use.

'Remember … … on that river cruise last summer?' he smiled.

'Of course, I do.' "Of course, I do." She spoke the words over her own.

Creating the Memory Loop had been a costly and time-consuming endeavour. She couldn't afford the fees of the ML Corp, so she'd paid a Street Looper. Guys who had the skills, but not all the swanky tech of MLC. It was still pricey. Black-market tech didn't come cheap; the Loopers, Docs and Modders had overheads too, y'know. She and the engineer had sat through hours of fragmented voice recordings; from Michael's workplace, submitted by friends, and family — at least those sympathetic to Serina's request. Original video and audio recordings worked the best. But some people had False Memories, FMs, created. The pitch, rhythm and cadence of the deceased's voice were easily copied using old deep fake tech. She had requested a couple of alterations; nothing much. When Michael had knelt to propose at a friend's dinner party, she'd spluttered, 'Are you for real?' The friend had recorded it. His response only needed the 'for' removed to give her a starter to her 'Memory'. It was a patchwork substitute at best. Her responses were then recorded. The editing was tedious. If you were lucky enough to have enough data, a whole day's worth of conversations could be reconstructed. She'd had her Memory Loop designed so that her voice was quieter than Michael's. Speaking the words out loud just felt more real. At the time, it was all she had wanted — the memories.

'You wore that....' Laugh. Blip. *'And then you bloody well jumped in the river. Wearing it!'*

'It was...'

'... dress.'

'Who cares?'

Blip. *'Of course, I'm real, honey.'* Back to the bloody beginning.

She yanked the jack free. Sat up, quick. Sobbing uncontrollably. God, she missed him so much, it hurt like physical pain. Shitty fucking technology. In two years, it had fragmented horribly. He's gone, gone, gone. Shitty waste. "It's not fucking fair!" she wailed at the unadorned walls.

It played on her mind. She continued her twelve-hour shifts. *Keep busy. That's the thing.* Was on her way to get her Memory Loop upgraded when she saw Frake again. She was drinking coffee outside one of the generic multi-national corporation outlets. Maybe she should go for the Physical Interactive Hologram? That way, she'd get to see him with her eyes open. Be able to interact with him, to a limited degree. But the prices were horrendous. A shadow fell across her pad. Glancing up, she saw a vaguely familiar face. Vaguely, because her memory of it was wobbly and distorted through an alcohol-fuelled haze.

"Hi," Frake raised a hand raised hesitantly. "Remember me?"

She nodded. He seemed relieved. They exchanged pleasantries. Small talk. And then, before she knew what was coming out of her mouth, she asked him about the museum. He told her that he had been visiting for six months. Since Laura had passed. He did it fortnightly. Was looking forward to his next one.

"What's it like?" she asked.

"Like nothing else."

"What d'you mean?"

"You know those Memory Loops?" he gestured to her forearm. "And those Interactive Holos? Better than that."

"Better? How?"

"Because they're *real*. It's *them*. Not a memory, or a copy. It *is* Laura." His excitement was evident. Infectious.

"Can't be. They're..." she couldn't say it.

"Dead," he whispered. She winced. "I know. I'm sorry. But believe me. I know my Laura. They found a way to contain the human soul."

It preoccupied her for days. *They found a way to contain the human soul.* She tried to keep busy. Worked more hours. Sought distraction. Visited late-night cinema shows to keep her from lying in bed — *their* bed. Drank too much. Paced her room, eyes darting to the holoportrait of him on her dressing table. *They found a way to contain the human soul.*

Finally, she drove out there.

The inside matched the exterior. Run-down, ill-lit. Cases lining the walls displayed bits and pieces from a bygone age. Radio parts. Components from digital devices. Part of a satellite dish. Gateway switches, faster than light transmission relays, and a 'multi-port power amplifier', whatever that was. One glass display stand held a torpedo-shaped thing. Sleek, silver, shaped like a dolphin without fins or tail. About the size of her forearm from elbow to wrist. 'Primary Connection', the exhibit label read. The impression was that someone had created an amateur exhibit of their private collection of junk. No wonder it was neglected. About to leave — what a waste of time, Frake had been screwing with her — she noticed a man sitting on a chair with his back against one wall, reading. No one else was in the museum.

Feeling nervous, stupid, she asked, "What is all this?" He told her it was all about communication.

"How marvellous," he said, "and baffling, that humans were able to create some of the most sophisticated communication hardware, and yet were unable to actually listen to one another. Let alone visitors." He waffled on about this piece and that to the point that she became irritable and bored.

"And this is it? I thought..." gesturing around the small room. He gave her an odd look. His eyes were the colour of moss in the dim lighting. Why had she come? he asked. Told him someone had recommended it. Was she disappointed? To be honest, yes. She had hoped for more. Maybe she was interested in their 'special' collection? She nodded solemnly.

A heavy door in the back wall. He keyed into a pad beside it. It slid open on well-maintained hinges. He ushered her through. Pleasantly cool, the lighting muted. The walls were painted a relaxing shade of deep blue. An unfamiliar sense of calm came upon her.

"Hello, can I help you?" A woman with vibrant green eyes smiled warmly.

There was nothing on the walls to indicate what the interior held, simply the words *Found Souls*, in a white, flourishing font above the slick reception desk. The smell of the previous room, the river and the dust were missing. In fact, there seemed an absence of odour. Reminded her of the ICU. She swallowed back the tears.

Still staring at the white words, said "Hi." What was she supposed to say? Felt like she'd been given access to a secret club; maybe this was true. Was she meant to offer a codeword?

"Please, take your time." The woman indicated a chair. Serena sat. "I'm the Museum custodian, and we aim to keep our customers, both parties, content." What the hell did she mean by that? Serina suddenly felt she had made a mistake. Looked around for hidden cameras. Was it an elaborate joke after all? The custodian continued, "I understand that, on your first time, you might be nervous. It's a tricky thing to get to grips with, isn't it?" She sat beside Serina. "Most people first come because it was recommended."

"I never heard of you before a couple of weeks ago," Serina said, guarded.

"We don't exactly advertise. We're a relatively new enterprise. Doctors Landro and Foyle wanted to be certain everything worked."

"Worked?"

"Of course. One wouldn't want to have contact with the deceased without assurances."

"Of course." Serina glanced around again.

"And we need to ensure everyone's safety."

"Safety? You mean it's dangerous?"

The woman smiled amiably. "No. Not if instructions are followed."

Alanna, the custodian, asked a huge list of questions, checking off responses on some hi-tech data device unfamiliar to Serina. Who had told her about the museum? Had she any medical conditions? Did she believe in an afterlife? How many friends did she have? Any living family members? Did she get on with her neighbours? Her age. Her weight. Her daily habits. How long ago had Michael been killed?

Once Serina had recovered and wiped her eyes with the proffered towelette, she was taken through a set of doors that whispered open, quiet as HushCabs seating. Down a short flight of steps, and into a large room of slim display cabinets. There were three other people in here, talking to whatever the cabinets held. Alanna left her alone, giving her time to reach a definite decision. Serina walked slowly to the nearest case. Inside was a holograph of a girl. About six years old, with short reddish hair and wearing silver dungarees. Serina watched her wave and then hopscotch forward, before jumping back to the start. Wave. Hop. Inside the locked glass door, a discrete plaque displayed the name, *Rebekka Wilmot*. Attached to it was a small, silver fish-shaped object about the size of her little finger. Two of the three other visitors sat at a different display and waved to an elderly man sitting on a riverbank, fishing. They each had a tiny 'fish' stuck to their right temple. They were having a conversation — this was *not* a hologram. At least if it was, Serina thought, it was a bloody brilliant one.

On one of the cases, she pressed a button on the plinth. Serina listened to a woman's voice describe how her life had changed since her brother had come back into her life. How the museum had helped the pain to go. She couldn't praise the staff enough. The third person spoke to her as he was leaving. He was the father of the soul over there — he indicated a young man, waving. The father's overjoyed words at receiving his son back struck her hard. The accident had destroyed the family, he told her, but the museum had healed it. He sang the praises of the doctors. Of the technology. Couldn't thank them enough for allowing him more time with his son. He seemed genuinely happy as he bade her farewell and left.

"The families kindly allowed us to exhibit their loved ones so that others can see the potential. Get a feel for what one will experience. They really don't mind if you interact with them." Alanna walked back into the room. "But most want to keep things private, understandably. Not everyone wants to share their discovery or join with their loved ones. Or they don't want to *yet*."

"You mean," Serina didn't know how to pose her question. "The souls of these people are, where? In those little things stuck on their temples? How? I don't understand. Haven't they gone to Heaven?" aware that she sounded like a kid. Felt the blush flare across her face and chest. Heaven. When did she, Serina Esther Cosgrove, ever believe in Heaven, or life after death in any form for that matter? *We live, we die, and that's the end. Isn't it?*

Alanna explained, in plain language. One's loved one's souls did go to the next place beyond here, wherever that was. Doctors Landro and Foyle had developed ways to tap into the *ethereal realm,* as she put it. Serina thought it sounded like bullshit. Communication technology had advanced beyond anything anyone could have suspected. Contact had been made accidentally, originally. And when the first souls came willingly, they saw it as a way to alleviate much loneliness and suffering in the world. *A way to make a fortune, more like,* Serina imagined.

"Think of it as an advanced Memory Loop," Alanna said. "Except they are with you, in real-time. Because the souls of the dead are untethered to a geographic location, they can actualise where we are."

"Like a hologram?"

"A thousand times better," Alanna affirmed. "Because they're with you like they were in life."

She didn't understand a lot of what the custodian spoke about. Serina swung from scathing scepticism to wanting to believe. Souls weren't real, she kept telling herself. But what if I'm wrong? What if it's true? What if she could have some 'real' time with Michael? Found herself babbling about the terrible assault. Attackers never identified.

"At the funeral, I just sat there thinking, 'It's not real. He can't be dead...'"

She felt strangely unburdened afterwards. The whole business seemed crazy. The custodian suggested a trial run. Free. *It's probably a new holo-tech*, Serina theorised. But decided, as it was a free offer, to see what it was all about. She went ahead and gave Michael's details to Alanna. She was given a Soul Relay Coil or SRC, as it was called, and instructions. Signed a contract that her eyes skimmed but her brain barely registered.

She was given a private room. Where she could 'meet', her Soul Mate again. Tastefully and simply decorated, it contained only two chairs and a short sofa. She took out the 'coil'. It came in two parts. Less coil, more fishlike, it was definitely metal, but it lay soft and light in her palm. Its outer surface was articulated so that it moved fluidly when she flexed her hand. The other side flat and a little slick to the touch. The second part, which went into her ear, was a pea-sized ball on a kind of rubber silicone earpiece. She reread the instructions and attached the earpiece. The other adhered to her temple, forming itself to the contours How the hell was this supposed to even create a hologram? She was still fairly certain that the whole thing was a hoax perpetrated to cash in on the bereaved.

"Hello?" She waited. "Are you there, Michael?"

Something whacked the side of her head. It went dark. When she opened her eyes, he was sitting on the sofa.

"Oh!" Was all she could manage.

"Hi, sugar."

Despite her incredulity, her uncertainty, Serina approached the image of Michael. He looked as he always had. Tentatively, half hopeful, half expecting her suspicion that it was all fake to be proved true, and readying herself for disappointment, she reached out. Her hand made contact. She snatched it back. Frightened and incredulous. He remained composed, waiting. Serina swallowed down the lump in her throat. Bit her thumb, hard. She was awake, they hadn't drugged her, as she'd begun to suspect. He tilted his head and raised his eyebrows. She dived forward, expecting him to vanish in a puff. Imagined. A dream. Her arms closed around his neck. She smelt his cologne. His hair was slightly musky from labouring at the factory. He was solid.

"Oh," her breath stilted, gasping. Thought she might faint. "Michael. It's really you?"

He embraced her the way he used to. Kissed the tip of her ear. "It's me, Serina. What took you so long?"

She cried in his arms for an age. They sat on the sofa, she awkwardly curled on his lap, her knees almost touching her chin, and talked. Not the Memory Loop conversation, but actual words. Remember that summer in Scotland? What a beautiful island. That terrible meal she cooked. Their first autonomous drive car, second-hand junk of course. The time they tried a stasis pod. She laughed until she cried.

"What's it like?" she finally asked.

Michael gave a little shake of the head. "That's something we can't do. Can't tell the living about the other side."

"There are rules in Heaven?" she laughed despite herself.

"Not exactly," he ran his thumb along her cheek, "I can't remember."

"Oh."

Serina had prepared herself for a short visitation — that's what Alanna called the connections to the souls. So, when it ended, she experienced sadness that Michael was not with her anymore, elation that such a thing was possible, but anticipation for next time. Deliriously happy, she returned the SRC and thanked Alanna. The custodian seemed delighted for her, pleased it had worked and that it had eased Serina's pain.

After her first 'freebie', she had hesitated about trying again. After the initial exhilaration had worn off, she had begun to question whether what she had experienced was an illusion. The logical portion of her brain argued that it was not real. The soul isn't real. It was simply super advanced technology. It happens all of the time. Scientists and engineers are always producing new things. *We live, we die, and that's the end.* But her heart said different. So, it was a while before she returned. Partly, she didn't care because this was definitely way better than the Memory Loop or any hologram she had experienced. It was time with Michael.

She visited every last Friday of the month, for four months. The next time she saw Frake, she thanked him for introducing her to the Museum. He was delighted at her newly rekindled relationship. Told her he was 'seeing' Laura twice a week. "You can feel their heart beating, can't you?" Expression animated. When she asked how come she never saw him at the Museum, he told her that he took Laura home. Serina remembered the cab drive; of course! he'd been holding his SRC then.

"How?" she exclaimed. Desperate.

He told her about the rental system. He said clients were encouraged to take their SRCs home. Gave you a longer connection. Of course, one had to pay more for it — like being a Platinum member of a club. How could he afford it? she asked. He had taken out a loan, several it turned out. Initially wary, she approached Alanna at the end of one of her museum visits and discovered that indeed Frake spoke the truth. Alanna said that Serina and Michael seemed to have made a positive and effective connection. That they were compatible. She did not elaborate, nor did Serina ask what she meant — of course she and Michael were compatible. They had been engaged to be married before his passing. Alanna suggested Serina put in a rental request. This would be reviewed, and a decision reached within the month.

The response was quicker than she expected. "It's to be back by five o'clock the day following use," Alanna said. Serina couldn't wait. It cost her three months' wages. But long hours for two years and no holidays had ensured her funds were sound.

Frake introduced her to a small, discreet group of people who were all soul users. Mostly 'Platinum' members of the museum. They explained how practice had extended the time spent with their loved ones. For seven months, she had returned her SRC on time. How did they manage it? Some had been users since the Museum began operation three years ago. They brushed her concerns aside. What could the custodian do about it once you had the coil? They paid for them, didn't they? Would the Museum send out the reclamation guys, or its version of them? Ha! At a later meeting, Serina was thrilled to learn that some of the group were able to spend whole nights or days with their dearly departed. Their enthusiasm was infectious. Their neurosis and edginess ignored. Moments of disillusion were explained away. Like when three of the members said that their dead spouses had been pressing them for more time together.

It took a few meetings to realise that the group was growing smaller. The long-term users no longer turned up. Then Frake heard that Samuel, the longest user, had been found in a coma in his apartment. It was sad, they agreed, but hadn't he looked ill for a while? Another had completely blanked Frake when he'd waved to her on the street. Like she didn't recognise him, he said.

The times spent with Michael were the best. Better than before, she told herself. How could this be? How could a soul be here, really? Ultimately, it didn't matter. It felt like they had been given a fresh start. It bore absolutely no comparison to the ML or a hologram. She could touch him, smell him. This was not a recording. This was Michael in the flesh. Often, he couldn't remember events she reminisced about. Sometimes his eyes seemed to look through, not at, her. But she did not care. She could hold him again. Kiss him. Properly. Not like the stupid Memory

Loop. Warm and heart-meltingly romantic in a way he had never been in life. He was, she believed, more amorous than when he had been alive. It was to be expected, she supposed, that someone who had experienced death and Heaven would have peculiarities. She ignored them all. She was more in love with Michael than she ever had been. She told herself it was because it was his soul she was with, the body thrown aside had left the best of him. He wanted to be with her more than ever. Talked of them staying together.

Serina seldom used the HushCabs canteen. A tiny room to the rear of the basement office in a multi-storey complex. Work had lost what little attraction it previously held. But she needed the money now. She poured coffee.

"Hasn't been seen for weeks." Kal leaned back on his chair. "Probably in a mental health lockup by now."

"You talk a lot of hooey," Pete said.

"It's true. They get addicted." Kal said.

"What's that?" Serina said, sitting next to Pete.

Pete shoved his pad into a pocket. Reached for his cab keycard, "Kal says a bloke he knows was communing with his dead missus. Claims he got some device or other from a shady customer, who said he could actually see her again. Can you believe that?" Pete guffawed and headed out.

Kal studied Serina over the rim of his mug. She avoided his gaze. "You know what I'm on about, don't you?" He placed the mug on the table, both hands wrapped around it.

"What d'you mean?"

"You didn't bat an eye when Pete told you. You didn't laugh."

"So?"

Kal regarded her some more. "Don't tell me you're onto it too. Serina! Please don't tell me you're 'in touch' with Michael," making air quotes. His expression slid from exasperation to concern.

She claimed not to know what Kal was talking about. Denied knowledge of the *fucking Soul device*, as he put it. Finally admitted that she had been in touch with her dead fiancé. Kal was furious. Called her stupid. Said she was meddling in things that she didn't understand. The bastards touting the idea couldn't understand.

"How can we," he gestured, all-encompassing, "have an inkling of the afterlife? How do we know where souls go, or what they are? We know nothing. And we shouldn't be meddling in their affairs, Serina!"

"But, Kal," she felt tears welling.

"It's some crackpot con by some bloody quack! Or worse."

"No. It's him. It really is. I didn't believe it at first, but —"

"Serina, listen to me, honey." He took one of her hands in his large, calloused ones. "I know it's terribly hard, especially for a young one like you. I know what it's like. I lost my Gina ten years back. Do I miss her? Every single day. Does it hurt? Absolutely. Would I like to see her again? Of course, I bloody would. But alive, honey. Not this mockery of a human soul, or whatever it is they're fobbing you off with."

"It is him. It's Michael. He remembers everything from his life, from our life together. It's not a mockery." She knew it wasn't true as she said it. Michael didn't remember everything. But wasn't that to be expected when a person had been dead two years?

Kal sighed and stood. "If you know what's good for you, you'll stay away from whoever deals with this tripe and try to carry on without him. It's what's natural."

After a whole intoxicating evening with Michael, Serina thought about what Kal had said to her. Nonsense. She and Michael were better than ever. Happier than before. His memory returned with each reminder. Michael had assisted her efforts to extend the time they spent together. Alanna had, surprisingly, been understanding about the late returns of the SRC. Of course, there was a surcharge, but she seemed remarkably flexible. Kal warned Serina it was addictive. Michael called Serina his addiction. Kal accused her of living in a fantasy. Michael confessed he believed they had been given a new chance. Kal talked about living with the pain of loss. Michael said they could be together forever. Kal told her there was no such thing as forever.

Michael said,

"I love you." He was perfect. "Don't return me tomorrow," he said.

Serina considered his suggestion as she sat outside the Museum, engine ticking over, the device in the palm of her hand. Hadn't seen Frake for months. The members of the group had dwindled to two; Serina and a bloke called Douglas. He said that the others had succeeded in permanently uniting with their loved ones. She recalled Kal's words in the canteen: 'Probably in the mental health lockup by now.'

She lay on her bed. Attached the Soul Relay Coil. Michael arrived instantly. Quicker each time, she noticed. His beautiful lips curved in a smile. His blue eyes shone green from the neon sign across the street.

"My love."

"Darling."

"Have you decided?" he whispered, lips brushing her ear.

Serina sighed. "I have. I will."

"You're sure? You want us to stay together forever?"

She kissed him passionately. "I do!" Michael lay down beside her. "Will it hurt?"

She closed her eyes and felt a sensation of something passing over her. Felt Michael's presence more intensely, growing, encompassing. Like he had lain on top of her and was sinking through her skin, her muscle, her bones. Deliciously intoxicating. She half opened her eyes. His face close above her. Concentrating.

Relax, she heard his voice in her head. I*t's easier if you just let go.* She shuddered as if jarred on a bumpy road. He was inside all of her, and she was being squeezed into a smaller and smaller part of herself. Could feel Michael's soul pressing hers down. A hint of panic. *Is this death?* she wondered. Soothing overtures. An invisible finger on her lips. *I'm disappearing.* Smaller and smaller. Saw blue sparks ahead, pulsing gently.

For some reason, she thought about the arcane communication debris she'd seen at the museum. The weird silver 'Primary Connection' exhibit. It was all about communication, the attendant said. *Or lack of.* She saw Alanna's green eyes as she said that they were compatible. Soul Relay Coil — the word Relay repeating in her dwindling mind. What did they mean by 'relay'? What was being relayed?

Michael's infiltrating tones. She hadn't listened. *We* hadn't listened. Relay. To pass on, to receive. All those things in space. All those unanswered signals that people said were stuff and nonsense. We just didn't listen properly.

Tendrils reached forth, tickling inside her head, making a connection. Momentarily, she and he were harnessed together. Two in one. *Relax, it's easier if you just let go.* But suddenly, felt like she was sliding down a water park slide. Corkscrewing into ever tighter circles. *Easier for whom?* came the thought. Realising, too late that Michael — no, not Michael, an interloper, a liar, *an other*, occupied her body. *They found a way to contain the human soul.* Who, the thought slipped like silk into her mind, were *They*? Green eyes passed before her; the attendant, the custodian. Michael. And her conscious mind, her soul, was entering the SRC.

She didn't even have a mouth with which to cry out.

See Alexandra Peel's story "Love, Death, and the Electric Soul" online at Metaphorosis.
If you liked it, leave a comment. Authors love that!
Remember to subscribe to our e-mail updates so you'll know when new stories are posted.

About the story

Love makes the world go around, or so they say. Love connects. Romantic love combined with pragma binds us. Death is common to us all, and yet can isolate individuals. The existence of a soul is still debated, in some circles.

I initially responded to the call for something about a museum. What — I wondered; would be the oddest thing a museum would house? What do we never see in museums and galleries? What, in fact, do we never see? The human soul. I knew it was going to be a futuristic piece immediately.

Then, I thought, but how can we see this elusive thing? Why on earth would anyone want to 'capture' it, display it, rent it out? There had to be an ulterior motive. I saw this clapped-out building in my mind. Nothing exciting — but what lay inside was going to change the lives of those who entered it in a way they could barely imagine. Then I imagined a person who does not believe in the soul, but they're in so much emotional pain, that they will grab onto anything to ease it.

Serina came fully formed, sitting in her taxi. Her fiancé is dead. She is alone in the world. Holograms and electronic memories don't cut it anymore for her. She desperately wants her fiancé back — and a chance meeting provides her with access to the museum's secret. I saw a photograph of the Allen Telescope Array in California, of the SETI institute and wondered what if 'they' have made contact — and we simply didn't understand? And decided to combine it with the very human — what would happen to someone who does not believe in an afterlife, or a soul, 'We live, we die and that's the end.' Serina says, who then encounters one — or does she?

A question for the author

Q: Is there a specific environment you find most conducive to writing, and is it different for different kinds of scenes?

A: These days I like silence. It's hard to come by what with the neighbours' dogs, shouting, music and so on. I often wear headphones and have some music playing very quietly to try and drown out extraneous noise. The music is always relevant to the story I am working on, so I research and make a short playlist each time. I have collections of film scores, sci-fi sounds, 17th century lute music, protest songs and Elizabethan pieces. I'm working in my daughter's old bedroom at the moment, which is painted white. The wall before me contains maps of the world I invented for a historical fantasy novel. Sketches of towns, an inset map, showing a detailed part of the map at a larger scale. And lots of sticky post-it notes. The from the window view is an uninspiring one of other people's houses — so I look at the sky above the roofs.

About the author

Alexandra is a visual artist turned author. She has a degree in Fine Art: Sculpture. She has been a freelance artist, community artist, graphics tutor and bookseller. She currently works as a Learning Support practitioner in a F.E/H.E college. She hails from the sunny island of Britain!

www.sticksandstonesbooks.com, @AlexandraPeel

Snowman

Han Whiteoak

Meltwater dripped from the snowman's carrot nose as he boarded the train. A soggy red scarf hung around his neck as he slid down the aisle like a melting glacier, leaving a glistening wet trail.

Alma elbowed her dad. "Look!"

Dad was skimming the headlines on his tablet. She knew without looking that they were bad — fires here or floods there. Gran, whom they were going to visit, would have been ranting about the state of the world, but Dad read quietly, giving only a little nasal sigh every now and again.

He sighed now as he glanced up. "Don't point, Alma. "It's rude."

As the snowman slid past Alma, she gave him an encouraging smile. With one twiggy hand, he stiffly raised his bobble hat at her. It settled back on his head as he headed for a seat behind them on the shady side of the train.

Alma, who had twisted around in her seat to watch, turned back to Dad. "Where's he going?"

"North, I guess."

"Why?"

"It still snows up there."

That morning, a freak snowstorm had delayed their train leaving the city. The passengers, stamping their feet on the platform, had complained. *Snow like the olden days*, they'd said. *So much for global warming.*

The train clunked back into motion. Outside the window, the snow was already melting, dripping from the early-budding trees. Alma pulled off her jumper and stuffed it under her seat. It was the first time they'd been to visit Gran since coastal flooding had damaged the railway line. There had been a lot of debate, which they'd followed closely through the TV, over whether the damage was worth repairing, as the same thing was likely to happen again. Dad had fretted, phoned Gran, fretted some more. "She's raging herself into an early grave over all this," he'd said. Finally, the track had been fixed, new defenses had been erected, and now they were on their way.

Alma kept sneaking glances at the snowman. She could remember only one winter where it had snowed enough to build one. Gran had tutted at Alma's inexperience and shown her how to roll the snow into a ball almost as big as herself. Gran had lifted a smaller ball on top to make the snowman's head, and hoisted Alma up so she could give him eyes and mouth and nose. Draping her favourite red scarf around his neck, Alma had whispered a promise to the snowman that they'd be friends forever. But by the following morning, he had melted to a pile of slush.

The snowman on the train quietly dripped. He pushed and pulled at the window, trying to open it. One twiggy arm splintered with the effort, leaving his hand dangling by a strip of bark. Half-melted, his mouth sagged to one side, like Gran after she'd fallen from the roof of the town hall, protesting for cleaner air..

The snowman needed help. And yet no one did anything. Dad was engrossed in the latest tragic news story, sighing and shaking his head. When she said, "Dad, do you think we should..." he put a finger to his lips without looking up.

Alma had promised to be good today. When Dad said be good, he meant she should be quiet and not trigger one of his headaches. But Gran said goodness was more than that. It was about helping people who needed it. Alma wasn't sure whether a snowman counted as people, but that part didn't seem as important as the part about the helping. Pulling a band from her plaited hair, she slid off her seat and approached the snowman, who turned to her with sad coal eyes.

"It's alright," she said. "I want to help."

He stared at her blankly. She pointed at his broken arm. He held it out. It was covered in scaly lichen, which scratched her fingers as she took his dangling hand and bound it as best she could.

A murmur hummed through the carriage. When Alma looked up, Dad was standing over her. "Leave it alone, love. Come and sit down."

She looked at the snowman, beads of water running down his head, and back at her father. "He's melting."

"I know, but there's nothing we can do."

Alma knew she shouldn't make a scene. But she couldn't ignore the snowman. With lots of help from her medical team, Gran had recovered, so that now her face was nearly symmetrical again. Surely the snowman could get better too?

She pulled herself up to her full height, the top of her head level with Dad's chest. "Gran says I should always help when I can."

Dad looked tired. When opened his mouth, Alma was sure he was about to order her to sit down, but then he said gently, "That's true. She does say that." He sighed. "Well, then. What should we do?"

Alma reached past the snowman and pulled open the window. The breeze sent the melted drops on the snowman's cheeks streaming back towards the seat. He didn't look any colder.

She thought for a moment. "We can get the train staff to turn the heating down!"

Newspapers rustled. Whispers hissed. Dad looked embarrassed.

"Excuse me," an old woman protested. "I've just taken off my coat."

"Can't you put it back on?" Alma said. "Look!"

The snowman's nose drooped. As his face softened, hollows opened around his eyes, which threatened to topple from their sockets. His hat slid from his head and landed soggily in the aisle. The other passengers pretended to be absorbed in phones or books.

"Very sad." The woman barely glanced at the snowman. "But what can I do?"

Alma glared and crossed her arms.

"Well, now," said an old man, whose dog had snatched up the snowman's hat and started chewing on it. "Perhaps we could take a vote."

Grown-ups never did anything without a lot of talking. Each person gave their opinion on the temperature in the carriage, and then repeated it, louder, when someone else disagreed. Frustrated, Alma fanned the snowman with her book. It didn't help.

"What's the point in talking about this?" said one passenger.

"We'd have to get all the other carriages to agree," said another. "It'll never happen."

"I don't think it's warm, anyway," said the old woman. She pulled her fur coat across her like a blanket and glowered over it, red-faced.

The discussion went round in circles. Every time the passengers neared agreement, someone piped up that the snowman didn't look so bad.

"It was dribbly when it boarded," said the old woman. "You can't blame us for that."

"Snowmen have always melted," said the dog owner. "It's natural."

"That's not true," said Alma.

But no one listened.

The snowman slumped against the window. He looked smaller than before. Couldn't they see this was urgent?

"Come on," Dad said. "This is our stop."

Alma looked out at the slushy platform. "Wait!" Gently, she cradled what was left of the snowman and carried him out. He was so shrunken that he weighed barely anything. She had to support his head so it didn't topple off his shoulders. His meltwater soaked her gloves.

They stepped onto the platform and made their way towards the station exit. Dad had his hand firmly on Alma's shoulder. He was looking around for Gran. Arms full of the snowman, Alma wiped her tears on her opposite shoulder.

The snowman was dripping through her fingers. She laid him on a drift beside the station entrance. Travellers stamped past, not caring.

"What's that?" said a voice. "You can't leave that there. It's littering."

Dad stepped between Alma and the station worker. "It's a snowman that was on the train. My daughter wanted to help."

"Aye, my kids are into all that too," the man said.

Alma ignored him. She straightened the snowman's buttons and dug his carrot nose into the snow so it stood upright. She took off her hat and laid it where the top of his head should be. He was so melted it was hard to tell, but she thought she saw a smile ripple across his face.

"Looks like he's had it," the man said. He sounded almost gleeful about it. "If you don't want to keep the bits as a souvenir, there's a bin over there."

Alma's hands balled into fists. She whirled around, ready to tell the man he was a heartless idiot, but caught sight of a hunched figure making her way across the car park, leaning on her stick.

"Gran!"

She ran over, wrapped her arms around the old woman's waist and, in sniffling sobs, told her the whole story. The station worker backed away as Gran turned her steely gaze on him.

"Now then," she said, once he'd gone. "Who have we here?"

The snowman was no more than a carrot, a blood-red scarf, and a few discarded lumps of coal.

"I'm sorry," Alma said. "I tried to help, but I failed."

"No," said Gran. "You didn't fail. You let him know someone cares. That counts for a lot."

"But he died. I couldn't even make the people on the train listen."

"Well," Gran said, straightening up to her full height. "Getting people to listen is harder than saving even one snowman. But that doesn't mean it's not worth a try."

"Mother..." Dad said.

"Hush," she said. "By the sound of it, you've been no use."

"I didn't stop her," Dad protested.

"Never mind not stopping her. What were you doing to help?" She took Alma's hand and started to lead her across the car park. "Now, I know a thing or two about making people listen."

Dad trailed along behind them, carrying their heavy bag. Alma snuggled into her grandmother's side, wiping her tears on the old lady's coat. She had the feeling they were about to start something important.

See Han Whiteoak's story "Snowman" online at Metaphorosis.
If you liked it, leave a comment. Authors love that!
Remember to subscribe to our e-mail updates so you'll know when new stories are posted.

About the story

When asked to write about the origins of "Snowman", I actually couldn't remember how the story started. After looking back through an old notebook, I realized that the original idea came from a *Furious Fiction* prompt:

- Your story must take place on a TRAIN.
- Your story must include something FROZEN.
- Your story must include three 3-word sentences in a row.

Furious Fiction accepts entries of up to 500 words which must be submitted two days after the prompts are released. The version I entered was much shorter and less well developed than the final story that appears in *Metaphorosis*. Alma, Dad, and Gran didn't appear at all. Instead, unnamed train passengers talked about the snowman but refused to help him.

Around the same time, I was taking a short story course taught by Emily Devane through the organisation Comma Press. Emily set a homework exercise to write about "an unexpected thing in a normal setting." I chose to keep working on this story, adding Alma and her father and bringing it up to around 900 words.

After a bit more reworking, I submitted Snowman to *Metaphorosis*. Editor B. Morris Allen liked it but pointed out that it was more of a mood piece than a story. During edits, Gran's role became much stronger. I realised she had a potential as a mentor and could be the catalyst to turn this emotional encounter with a snowman into a life-changing event for Alma.

I'd always thought of this story as a climate change metaphor, with the snowman as the "elephant in the room" that everyone was determined to ignore. One goal during edits was to make this theme more obvious.

A question for the author

Q: How do pets/children/significant others help/hinder your process?

A: Not having a partner, children or pets frees up time for writing, although I often give in to the urge to take a break and go to the park where I can watch other people's dogs run around happily. My best friend, who is a big fan of the *Metaphorosis* podcast, is always happy to read my stories and discuss them in detail. However, as he knows me so well, he often predicts plot twists or understands what I mean even when I've explained it badly. I'm in a couple of writing groups so I can get a range of feedback.

About the author

Han Whiteoak is a speculative fiction writer living in Sheffield, England. They have a degree in physics, a passion for the Peak District, and an incurable habit of borrowing more library books than it is possible to read during the loan period.

www.hanwhiteoak.me, @hanwhiteoak

Infinite Possibilities

Michael Gardner

A mystery USB leads Adrian to a cabin, where Other Adrian appears on an old television. Other Adrian is a version of himself from a parallel world. He encourages Adrian to build a machine that will facilitate travel to Other Adrian's world. Other Adrian informs him that his agent will be in contact.

Adrian has just found out his wife, Candice, is having an affair. He meets Other Adrian's agent, who turns out to be a woman, Taylor, that Adrian had a brief relationship with years ago. Taylor convinces him to confront Candice about her affair, and to go with Taylor to Other Adrian's world.

Adrian fights with Candice. He completes the machine, and with Taylor, leaves Candice to return to the cabin.

4

As Taylor inserts her key into the padlock, Adrian glances back over the canola toward the housing estate, and Taylor's car parked on the verge of the empty road. Night has fallen, but the moon is full, and casts the scene in a soft, silvery glow. There is no wind. It's almost as if the world is holding its breath with anticipation. It makes Adrian nervous. Hairs raise on his arms, his heart quickens.

He turns back to see Taylor slide the chain from the gate and drop it to the ground. She pushes the gate inward, waits for Adrian to enter.

The machine is deceptively heavy, seemingly getting heavier the longer he carries it. His forearms burn. He moves with quick, stuttering steps up onto the deck. He has to wait again for Taylor to catch up, to open the cabin door. Inside, nothing has changed. Thick wooden walls, the old kitchenette, the metal bed frame at one end. In the middle of the room is the television on the stand, the rug, the armchair. A slice of suburbia in a nineteenth century cabin.

He can't hold the machine any longer. His arms are numb. He lurches inside, half places, half drops his creation onto the rug.

"Careful," Taylor exclaims. She's quickly at his shoulder, running a hand over the casing like it's a wounded pup. He rises, steps back from it.

"Sorry," he says, wondering why he's apologising.

Taylor's face softens, and she opens her mouth to say something, but the words remain unsaid as her eyes dart toward the television screen. Adrian follows her gaze, and finds it warming up. What was black is now blue and backlit. Shadows resolve into recognisable forms. A thick neck, glasses, pursed lips—Other Adrian's face. And filling the background, strange fleshy protrusions that rise and fall rhythmically, like a sick animal breathing raggedly, but no animal Adrian has ever seen. The room is filled with them. Veined, monstrous masses, shuddering. It makes Adrian feel sick. What the fuck are they? His mind can't process the images.

"You're both here, good," Other Adrian says, commanding Adrian's focus. He swallows. The image on the television zooms, and Other Adrian's face fills the screen.

Taylor takes his hand, and he looks down to see his calloused hand wrapped in her slender fingers. His mouth is dry.

"I see you've completed the machine. Not far from the tree, Adrian," he says, the hint of a smirk on his lips. "Is it operational?"

Before Adrian can answer, Taylor jumps in. "Yes. He's tested the receiver."

Adrian's brow furrows. Her tone is sharp, the husk gone, replaced with an authority he doesn't recognise.

"Show me," Other Adrian says, and Taylor reaches for the machine, but Adrian shakes himself from his fugue and grabs at her wrist, stopping her.

"No, wait. I have more questions. I... I..." What? he thinks. "I'd like to hear again what you are offering."

Other Adrian's eyes move from Taylor to Adrian. He sighs—a disappointed school principal. "We've been through that," he says. Then silence.

Adrian tries again. "Well, what about where you are taking us? What is your world like?" he asks, his eyes darting to the flesh behind Other Adrian. "And how does bringing us there help you discover more about the universe? I'm not a scientist, I'm not smart. And Taylor? You said nothing of her last time—"

"I told you my agent would be in contact."

"Yes, but how did you contact her?"

"We don't have time for this." Then, to Taylor. "Start the receiver."

Taylor pulls free of Adrian. "Don't worry," she says. She looks certain, calm. But why would she be? She leans over and switches the machine on. It starts to hum, and he feels the vibrations of it in his skin, in his bones, his brain. His legs go weak.

"But how do you know?" he croaks, his voice not sounding like his own. Is it happening already? Taylor places hands on his shoulders, guides him backward. He wants to resist, but his legs won't obey. They move of their own accord. His heart feels like it's pumping gelatine. He bumps up against the armchair, his knees go, and he slumps into the chair.

"There you go," Taylor says, placing his useless arms in his lap. She holds two fingers against his wrist, and Adrian realises she's taking his pulse.

"What are you doing?" he drawls. His tongue is fat, useless. The saliva's gone, but his eyes water. There's pressure behind them. He looks from Taylor to the television, where Other Adrian grins. Behind him, the tissue is throbbing. It seems to be synchronised with the vibrations of Adrian's machine.

"Why did you need me to build the receiver?" he asks. He wrestles for control of his head, his eyes, he forces them to move to Taylor. "You said Other Adrian sent the television, this chair, the book. So why not just send a receiver?"

He hears a wet, gurgling sound from Other Adrian that he first mistakes as coughing, but realises is laughter. "Oh, finally. You're putting it together. Not as stupid as I suspected."

"The field doesn't support complex machinery," Taylor says. "Only organic matter and inanimate objects." And then, to Other Adrian, "His pulse is steady, breathing normal. Proceed."

Normal, he thinks. His breathing sounds like a jet engine in his ears. His heartbeat is erratic. The air in the room is hot. It's crushing him. Yet none of that is the odd thing, his mind says through the ooze. Why is she reporting to Other Adrian? And then he understands.

"He sent you. You made the modifications to the television once you arrived."

She turns, looks at him coldly. "Yes. And you made the receiver to bring us back."

"You said you were a local historian. You knew about our past."

"Yes."

"You lied?"

"No. Taylor, your Taylor, was a local historian. I found her here. She was... generally cooperative."

"Where is she now then?" he asks.

"With me," she says, tapping her temple.

He doesn't understand. None of this makes sense. He can hear something else now. A squelching. Like the sound of fish slapping against the bottom of a boat. But large fish. Many of them.

And then he feels pressure everywhere, like he's been encircled by the coils of a monstrous python, which squeezes. But the flesh of this snake is warm, not cold. It has fine hairs that tickle his neck and arms, and it is slick with a rancid-scented sweat that makes him want to retch.

He cranes as far as his uncooperative neck allows, but there's nothing behind him. The sensation of something squeezing him remains, though.

There's a jolt, and suddenly he feels like he's in two places at once. The cabin, as well as the room on the other side of the television screen.

"I don't want this," he moans.

There is that phlegmy sound again, Other Adrian's laughter. "Buyer's remorse, that is all. But I promise you, you will be better off here with us."

And as afraid as he is, he wonders. Maybe he's right. Without Candice, what's left? Drifting through life, driving the bus, ignoring a wife that fucks other men?

He sees Candice. She's crying, she's guilty, she's angry. She's trying to get him to pursue university, to find a better career, to take more shifts at work. She's trying to get him to have a little fun, to solve a puzzle that arrived in the post. A puzzle that she thought was a simple game, something that he might enjoy, which turned out to be much more. And yet as he relives that day again, the day he held the USB in his hands, he sees her anew, like he's floating out of body watching them both. She encouraged him. She's always encouraged him. If she doesn't love him, why do that? Why bother? To assuage her guilt? He doesn't buy that.

He hears her voice in his head. No, not in his head. He wrenches his gaze toward the door. Candice is there, eyes wide, pale in the moonlight, her mouth agape.

"What the fuck is..." but she doesn't finish.

"What's she doing here?" Other Adrian growls onscreen. Taylor lunges, and Adrian tries to get his swollen tongue to cooperate long enough to warn her.

But he doesn't need to. She's never really needed him, he realises, and this is no different. While he's still forming the words, Candice steps toward Taylor, not away. He sees her pull her arm back, and then she swings what appears to be one of his shifter spanners hard into Taylor's face. There's a sickening crack, and Taylor's head snaps back, and she collapses at Candice's feet with a heavy thud.

Candice, still brandishing the shifter, shakes. She's looking at Taylor's prone form, then at the screen, then Adrian pinned to the armchair. Her whole body shivers like a mirage.

"It's you," she says so quiet that Adrian almost doesn't hear her. "It's you there... but also..."

"That's not me," are the words he forces from his throat.

She stares at him, her face a ball of worry and confusion. "Adrian?" she asks.

And he's never been so glad to hear his wife say his name. He tries to smile, hopes it doesn't look grotesque. Suddenly their problems seem non-existent. A trifle that he turned into something insurmountable. He's never felt such relief.

From the television screen comes a grunt of annoyance. "Enough," says Other Adrian. There is motion there. Adrian feels a sharp jolt like he's riding a rollercoaster into a vertical loop, g-forces slamming his head against the headrest. It's hard to keep his eyes open.

From Candice, he hears his name again, but it's garbled. He tries to tell her to switch the receiver off. He's not sure he's successful. He feels hands on his shoulders shaking him. He hopes it's her. There's a slap to his face, but it feels distant, and oddly cold, which is nice given the humidity in the air, and the fever heat of the flesh that enfolds him.

He hears Candice's voice once more. Then everything goes black.

The worst thing Adrian ever did was stop Candice seeing her mother the night she died. It wasn't intentional, yet intention didn't change the end result.

He thought Alexia had been getting better. The chemo seemed to have halted the spread of the cancer, and Alexia, over those last few days, had a little more energy. It was Alexia that suggested that he take Candice away for the weekend. A break from work. A break from sickness.

Candice didn't want to go. She wanted to stay close to her mother, just in case. Truth was, Adrian had grown jealous of Alexia over the course of her illness. The majority of Candice's time was allocated to her, not him. It made him wonder how she would be if they had a child. Yet he comforted himself that that would be different. That would be investing time in life, not death. A terrible thought, he knew. But that was what he thought.

He spent more than they could afford
to rent an apartment by the beach. He
wanted to take Candice near the water so
they could try for that kid with the sound
of the waves in their ears. A throwback to
their first years dating at university, their
make-out spot in a mostly empty carpark
right on the far end of the main beach. He
couldn't recreate it exactly, but he wanted
the sound.

The car was packed, ready to go, when
Alexia called. Candice picked up after one
ring and smiled as she said hello. But as
Adrian watched, that smile became a
straight line, then a frown. She listened
for a long time, then offered to come over,
which shouldn't have irritated Adrian as
much as it did. But it did. He swallowed,
turned away and rapped his fingers on top
of the car. Candice glanced at him,
shrugged apologetically, listened.

"Okay, Mum. Love you. Bye."

She'd barely hung up the phone when
he jumped in, impatient. "What's up?" he
asked, staring across the roof of the car.

Candice shook her head, bit her
bottom lip, sighed. "She's having nose
bleeds, and she's dizzy."

"Oh," he said. He couldn't think of
what else to say.

"She says she's okay, she just couldn't find her painkillers..." Candice said, trailing off.

"Well, if she's okay—"

"I don't think she is. She sounded... a little spacey. Her painkillers are in the cupboard over the sink, like they always have been." Candice stepped toward the car, stopped, looked at Adrian. "I think something's wrong. I think we should cancel. We can go next week—"

"Honey," Adrian said. He regretted his tone, but continued anyway. "Alexia's a grown woman. She knows how she feels. I know she's sick, but you're jumping at shadows."

Candice cleared her throat, opened her mouth to say something, but then closed it again without speaking.

"It was her idea, remember? She wants you to have some time to relax. Plus, we're only two hour's drive away. Not far, really. You deserve this. Stop feeling guilty."

She hesitated, then nodded. "You're right. She'd tell me, wouldn't she?"

"Of course, honey." He desperately wanted to get going before it got dark. But he didn't risk pushing her more than he had. He watched her thinking.

"Okay. But I might give her a call in an hour, if you don't mind."

"Of course not. In fact, why don't you call her when we get there, as well?"

She smiled, a sad smile, but a smile nonetheless. She opened the car door and slipped inside. He felt a pang of guilt, a tightness in his belly that gripped him for a moment, but then passed. He wasn't being selfish, he told himself. This was about more than just his enjoyment. It was about their chance to create a family. He slid into the driver's seat, reached over and squeezed Candice's leg. She held her phone tightly in both hands. She looked at him, smiled again. He closed the door with a bang, started the engine, and headed off.

An hour later, when Candice tried to call, they'd hit the mountains and couldn't get reception. So she had to wait until they arrived in the seaside town.

It wasn't Alexia who answered. It was a nurse. She explained that Alexia had called the ambulance, and she'd been admitted to hospital. Her nosebleeds hadn't stopped, and she'd taken a turn. They were doing tests.

Candice was frantic, insisting that they return that night. To his eternal shame,

Adrian argued against it, which resulted in her screaming at him.

He relented, eventually, and the trip was conducted in silence. Hers in fear, his in anger.

Alexia passed before they got home.

Adrian wakes to a sensory assault unlike anything he's ever experienced before. Blinding white light. The din of a thousand people talking simultaneously. The scent of ozone, burnt hair. The taste of metal. Cold, and heat. The sharp pain of tiny cuts, followed by tender caresses.

For a time all he can do is freeze, grit his teeth, sweat and hope the feelings disperse. He's a cat encircled in a towel; he doesn't know which way is up, down, or where to head for relief.

Slowly, the cacophony of stimuli dulls. It's still there, but manageable. Which allows him to assess his environment more thoroughly. He quickly identifies greater problems.

What he thinks of as light, he realises he can't actually see. What he thinks of as sound is beyond audible, a presence in his mind, a radio signal through the airwaves, and him the receiver. Taste, touch, scent—all of these things feel intensely familiar, yet different. Non-physical. It's like he's floating in amniotic fluid, inside a giant womb. Yet everything is floating, his insides, his outsides, his thoughts.

He tries to run his hands over his body to soothe his panic, but finds nothing. No body, no hands. He tries to scream, but no sound comes forth. Something creeps into his mind. A whisper: "Adrian."

More panic. He gags on the taste of copper. It recedes, and he back-pedals from the brink of insanity.

"Who... who is that? Where am I? What..." he was going to ask what happened to Candice, but then he remembers. He recalls Other Adrian on the screen, the receiver messing with his head, his body. He felt squeezed, drawn away. But where too? This isn't the other world he was expecting.

"You're in his realm, like all of us," says a voice that feels like his own, but isn't. "Physically subsumed, mentally joined. Part of a hive mind now, but controlled by —"

"—ourselves—" interrupts a second voice.

"—not   ourselves.   Nothing   like ourselves. He's—" comes a third.

"—evil—"

"—manipulative—"

"Other Adrian," Adrian projects.

There's a chorus of voices then, murmuring agreement reflecting back at Adrian the rightness of his description. The voices all sound like him, he thinks: the cadence, the tone, the feel of them.

"You said subsumed," Adrian interjects. The throng hushes slowly, like a crowd at the theatre as the curtains open.

"Yes, bodily subsumed. You can feel it if you concentrate. Reach out and we'll guide you." The voice pauses, waits. Adrian complies, and searches for his physical body; he reaches out with his mind for his hands, his feet, his chest and...

He falls into his body and is instantly crushed by a huge weight. He's damp, hot, surrounded by darkness. He feels intense pressure, then relief, then pressure, like his body is being gummed by a toothless giant. There's no pain as such, but even in his anesthetised state he knows his bones are breaking, and his organs are turning to jelly.

He jerks back hard, finds himself in the white space again. "What the hell?" he hisses.

"Yes, unpleasant."

"But that's impossible, I…"

"Impossible in your world. Impossible in mine as well."

Many more murmur agreement.

"But there are infinite worlds and infinite possibilities. Not all follow the same laws as each other."

Another Adrian chimes in. "In this world, it is better to think of Other Adrian as a large amoeba. An amorphous, creature, able to subsume others into itself. To grow stronger, larger, to learn."

"To feed. On the flesh—"

"—and our minds."

The Adrians allow Adrian a moment to process this. Instead, he pictures Candice coming home from work, finding him at his workbench. She always engaged him first. With small talk, a touch on his shoulder, something. Always first. He'll never have that again.

He's hit by the weight of his stalemate life. Neither moving forward, nor back. Floating. Resenting Candice for pushing him. Pushing him, he sees now, just to live a little more. He could have chosen to do so many things. He thought he'd chosen her. He thought she'd failed him, finding someone else. But it was him, he realises. He begrudged her for changing, for trying new things, for going after her career, for meeting new people, for trying to drag him with her. He begrudged her for mourning her mother. And for putting her grief before his desire for a family. How hadn't he understood this before? He wonders why she stayed.

All of this rushes through his mind like a man given news of a terminal diagnosis. A man forced to reassess his life, knowing it will end soon, and the time to fix his mistakes is insufficient.

"Candice," he thinks, and it's so plaintive, so quiet, he wonders if they even hear. But their murmuring suggests they do. And that they understand.

"Most of us lost her. Nearly all of us."

"But Other Adrian said Taylor was our soulmate."

"Lies," hisses another.

"But don't give up."

"No, don't give up."

"Infinite worlds with infinite love stories better than our own."

Adrian hopes that is true.

"And with your arrival, a final hope."

Adrian's attention is honed, he focusses in on the presence that said those words. "Hope?"

"Yes, hope. But we must act fast. He'll return soon."

"Act? To do what?"

"To overwhelm Other Adrian."

"I don't understand. How?"

"Some of us have been with him for a very long time. Studying, watching, waiting."

"We have found a chink. When he feeds, he exhibits—"

"—weakness. He becomes distracted. When he brings a new Adrian across, for a few moments only, he loosens the tight hold on us, focusses instead on the consummation."

"We've waited."

"Building our forces."

"He's been too powerful for us, as many of us as there are."

"Until now."

"Until now."

"We think."

"We hope."

"We're sure."

"If we all work together."

"We can wrest back control from him, and—"

"Candice. Can I see Candice again?" Adrian asks, desperate.

There is a swell of voices, and hurried discussions.

"Perhaps. But we must act now. Are you ready?"

"I don't even know—"

But he doesn't finish. The light is suddenly rushing by like he's riding the nose of a bullet train tearing through a white-lit tunnel. He's pushed flat against a surge of movement behind him. Screaming in his ears, a roar. He screams himself.

He slams hard into something that feels like a solid wall of steel. He disintegrates.

Adrian blinks, and is shocked to find he has eyelids again. The physical sensation of them feels strange after a period of having nothing.

But this body is not his own.

It's bulky, monstrous. He fills the room, each part of him pressing against the floor and the walls. There's humid air on his naked skin, and sweat oozes from his pores. The floor is slippery beneath his mass.

He's slumped over a bank of machinery, hands caressing a keyboard marked with odd symbols. His arms are stunted, a contrast to the rest of him. Intuitively, like being fed answers through an earphone, he knows that the machine before him controls the receiver that he built back home. But it also controls numerous other receivers in numerous other worlds.

Something hits him hard from behind like a truck mowing down a deer. There are voices in his head, screeching. Then Other Adrian speaks, his voice close and angry: "You ungrateful vermin, get out of my—" but the threat is cut short, the pressure eases. Adrian is in control again.

He pushes his monstrous torso upright. It's hard work. He can feel Other Adrian just behind a thin veil, fighting, but being held for the time being by Adrian's brethren. Yet Other Adrian still seems to retain enough will to make control difficult. Adrian feels like he's pushing a laden shopping trolley with a broken wheel. It won't let him go straight; it pulls him into displays of food, passing shoppers.

"What have you done with him?" demands Candice. Her voice sounds crackly, far away. He stares at a monitor affixed to the wall, and sees her on the screen, in the cabin, an empty armchair behind her.

He smiles at the sight of her.

"Don't grin at me, you smug prick. Answer me."

"Candice," he says, but the voice is not his own. It's deeper, gruffer. "It's me. This thing I'm in, this version of me, he brought me to his world, but I'm fighting back. I'm in him, but it's me."

Candice steps toward the screen, grimaces. She brandishes the large spanner still. Behind her he sees Taylor motionless on the floor. He wonders if she is still alive. Knowledge falls into his mind like rain on parched earth. He understands that Other Adrian was in the process of using the receiver to bring Taylor back next. The machinery has locked on, and will soon pull her into this world.

"Is this a joke?" Candice hisses. "Is this a fucking joke?"

There's not enough time to explain properly or convince her of who he is. He tries anyway.

"We used to go to the beach. The car park at the south end, late at night, where we'd smoke weed and talk about our futures. We both had huge dreams, but only one of us followed through. I broke our bargain, Candice. I never realised till now. But I did, and I'm sorry."

He watches her face waver, uncertain. The angry thin line that is her mouth falls into a frown. "How do you know this?"

"It's me, baby. I'm sorry. I know why you did what you did. I drove you to it through my selfishness. My inactivity. I should have done more to keep us close. I should have worked harder, at least on that one, important thing. I should have worked at us."

He feels on the brink of tears. He sees Candice's eyes moisten too. She opens her mouth, closes it. He doesn't know if she really believes it's him. But after a moment, the words flow from her like a torrent.

"I'm so sorry. I'm so, so sorry. I had no right. I know it doesn't matter, but I didn't love him. I never did. It was always you, I..." she starts to sob.

"I know, Candice. I do. It's just I've been too stupid to return the love you deserve."

A jolt forces him into blackness. He feels hundreds of presences slithering over each other like snakes, one larger, and more powerful than the rest—a python hissing, biting, writhing. But then the masses prevail, and overwhelm it once more. He opens his eyes to see Candice's worried expression.

"I don't have much time," Adrian says.

"Come home. Please come home, for me."

He taps into the collective minds of all the Adrians and confirms his suspicion. His shoulders slump. He feels an aching emptiness in the pit of his huge belly, like an icy vacuum. He shakes his head slowly. "I can't," he says, his voice a rasp. Candice sobs louder.

He wipes roughly at the tears that have fallen on his cheeks, then runs his hands over the keyboard, knowing instinctively what controls to issue.

There is a dull thumping sound, and Taylor is suddenly in the room, unconscious, face down on the wet floor.

"I'm glad of the time we had," he says to Candice. She's still crying, but watches him intently. "Even though I wasted so much of it, you were what made life worthwhile."

Michael Gardner   Metaphorosis

He feels the sea breeze as she holds his hand. Their feet are up on the dash of his car as they look out at the clear night sky and listen to the rhythmic sound of waves crashing.

"Please don't go," she whispers.

"I wish I didn't have to. But I do. There's more of us out there, Candice. Infinite versions of us, in different states of being. Some yet to meet, some deeply in love, some just starting out, like we did once, with all the promise of a lifetime to come. I can't let him take that from all of them."

"What about us?" she implores.

The cold in his stomach spreads through his limbs. He can barely choke out the words: "I love you."

He sees her next to him in the hospital when he wakes. He feels the ache as he sits with her at her mother's funeral, unable to take the hurt away. He sees the glint in her eye, the devilish smile on her lips as they make love. He sees her watching him as he works at his bench. Just watching, trying to decipher his thoughts.

The Adrians feed him what he needs.

His hands work quickly. Practiced hands flipping switches, typing instructions. He tunes out Candice's anguish as he works, but glances toward her occasionally, trying to keep her in his mind.

He engages all the receivers at his disposal. There are so many, in so many worlds. He doesn't need to wait for any of them to lock onto targets. Not for this task. He just needs them open. He initiates the dimensional transporter, the device Other Adrian used to send Taylor, the armchair, and the rug to him. He refocusses it, and along with the receivers creates a lengthy, complex loop.

"Goodbye, Candice," he says.

Other Adrian smashes through the defences of the Adrians, slams into him and squeezes. "What the fuck have you done?" he cries into Adrian's head, and out loud. "What the fuck—"

But it's too late.

The transporter makes a sound. A tick, tick, tick, then it pauses a beat. Whoosh.

Adrian can still feel Other Adrian's monstrous body. He feels the agony as its fat leg is sucked from the room, wrenched from its body, spat out in another world, only to be returned a second later, reduced to gore and splatter.

A slice of his shoulder and arm are gone, exposing bone. Other Adrian screams. Part of its stomach next, viscera slithering to the floor.

The receivers continue to send the parts back—shredded flesh, the stink of broken insides, shards of bone and blood raining down like a thunderstorm of red.

Adrian senses relief all around. He senses elation and celebration. He's not alone here at the end. And while he can't see Candice anymore, he has her firmly in mind.

Their vessel shudders, jerks. Torn and shredded. Crunched and diminished. Other Adrian wails like a spoilt child, but it's too late for him.

Adrian binds with the others, and they comfort him, and he them. They each share memories of their lives, recollections of love, and Candice.

He shares one memory. A memory of him and Candice locked in each other's arms, their whole lives ahead.

And then it ends.

*See all the installments of Michael Gardner's
story "Infinite Possibilities" online at
Metaphorosis.
If you liked it, leave a comment. Authors love
that!
Remember to subscribe to our e-mail updates so
you'll know when new stories are posted.*

Copyright

Title information

Metaphorosis December 2022

ISSN: 2573-136X (online)
ISBN: 978-1-64076-242-8 (e-book)
ISBN: 978-1-64076-243-5 (paperback)

Copyright

Works of fiction

This book contains works of fiction. Characters, dialogue, places, organizations, incidents, and events portrayed in the works are fictional and are products of the author's imagination or used fictitiously. Any resemblance to actual persons, places, organizations, or events is coincidental.

All rights reserved

Moral rights asserted

Each author whose work is included in this book has asserted their moral rights, including the right to be identified as the author of their respective work(s).

Publisher

Metaphorosis
a magazine of | speculative fiction

Metaphorosis Magazine is an imprint of
Metaphorosis Publishing
Neskowin, OR, USA

www.metaphorosis.com

Discounts available

Substantial discounts are available for educational institutions, including writing workshops. Discounts are also available for quantity purchases. For details, contact Metaphorosis at metaphorosis.com/about

Metaphorosis Publishing

Metaphorosis offers beautifully written science fiction and fantasy. Our imprints include:

Metaphorosis Magazine
Plant Based Press
Verdage
Vestige

You can also find us:
@MetaphorosisMag, @Metaphorosis
www.facebook.com/metaphorosis

Help keep Metaphorosis running by supporting us at
Patreon.com/metaphorosis

See more about some of our books on the following pages.

Metaphorosis Magazine

Metaphorosis

a magazine of speculative fiction

Metaphorosis is an online speculative fiction magazine dedicated to quality writing. We publish an original story every week, along with author bios, interviews, and notes on story origins.

We also publish monthly print and e-book issues, as well as yearly Best of and Complete anthologies.

Come and see us online at magazine.Metaphorosis.com.

Plant Based Press

plant
based
press

Vegan-friendly science fiction and fantasy, including anthologies of the year's best SFF stories, from 2016-2020.

Chambers of the Heart
speculative stories
by
B. Morris Allen

A heart that's a building, a dog that's a program, a woman sinking irretrievably — stories about love, loss, and movement.

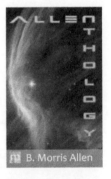

Susurrus

A darkly romantic story of magic, love, and suffering.

Allenthology: Volume I

Including three full collections of SFF stories.

Verdage

Science fiction and fantasy books for writers — full of great stories, often with an additional focus on the craft of speculative fiction writing.

Reading 5X5 x3

Changes

How do stories move from 'maybe' to published?

Here are 15 case studies of stories published in *Metaphorosis* magazine.

Reading 5X5 x2

Duets

How do authors' voices change when they collaborate?

A round-robin of five talented science fiction and fantasy authors collaborating with each other and writing solo.

Including stories by Evan Marcroft, David Gallay, J. Tynan Burke, L'Erin Ogle, and Douglas Anstruther.

Score

an SFF symphony

An anthology with an emotional score from the heights of joy to the depths of despair – but always with a little hope shining through.

Reading 5X5

Five stories, five times

See how different writers take on the same material.

Reading 5X5

Writers' Edition

Two extra stories, the story seed, and authors' notes on writing.